Dragonia

Revenge of the Dragons

Craig A. Price Jr.

CLAYMORE
PUBLISHING

Cover Design by Mariah Sinclair @ TheCoverVault.com

Editing by Tamara Blain @ ACloserLookEditing.com

Formatting by Craig A. Price Jr.

Dedicated to Albert Price,

I miss you grandpa. Thank you for always believing in me.

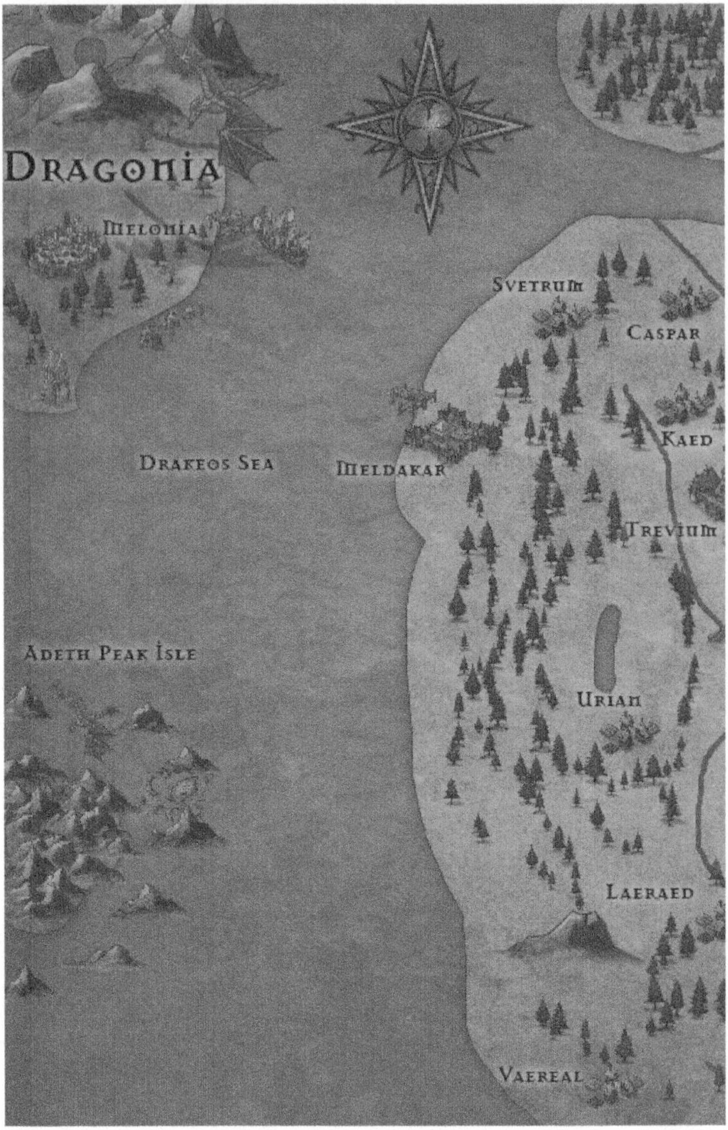

Dragonia

Melonia

Svetrum

Caspar

Kaed

Drakeos Sea

Meldakar

Trevium

Adeth Peak Isle

Urian

Laeraed

Vaereal

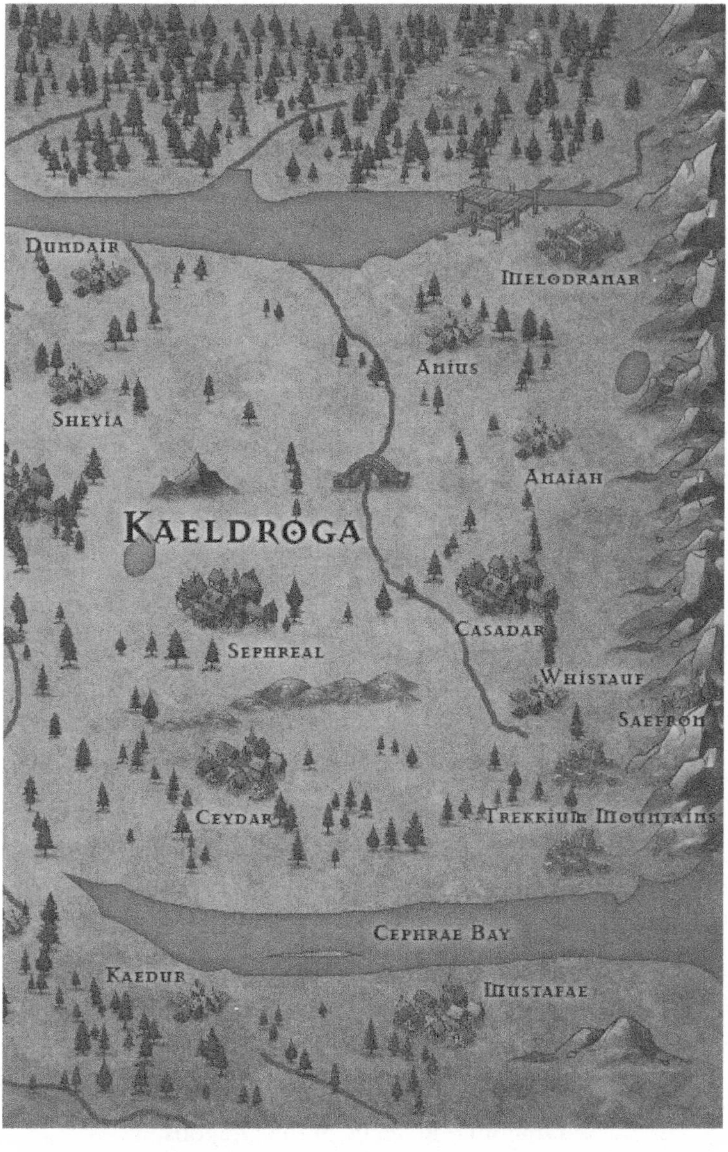

DUNDAIR

MELODRANAR

ANIUS

SHEYIA

ANAIAH

KAELDROGA

CASADAR

SEPHREAL

WHISTAUF

SAEFRON

CEYDAR

TREKKIUM MOUNTAINS

CEPHRAE BAY

KAEDUR

MUSTAFAE

Also By Craig A. Price

<u>Calthoria Shorts</u>
Chronicles of Starlyn
Heart of Ikchani
Victoria's Grave

<u>Claymore of Calthoria Trilogy</u>
The Crimson Claymore
The Obsidian Arrow
The Violet Flamberge

<u>Dragonia Empire</u>
Dragonia: Rise of the Wyvern
Dragonia: Revenge of the Dragons
Dragonia: Dragon Stone (Coming Soon)
Dragonia: Rise of Magic (Coming Soon)

Dragonia: Fall of the Dragons (Coming Soon)

Short Stories
Mage and the Freckled Frog
Diamonds Under a Hickory Tree

Anthologies
Fantastic Creatures
Glimpses
Pieces: A Mobile Writers Guild Anthology

More info:
http://Www.CraigAPrice.com/novels.html

EMPOWERING WOMEN? WOMEN wanting to break away from the male-led government? Read more about these amazon women called the Ikchani in my novella based in the same world as The Crimson Claymore and The Chronicles of Starlyn.

You can get it FREE Here[1]

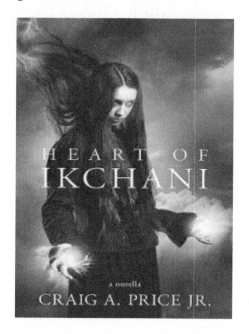

AS AN INDIE AUTHOR, reviews[2] are really important to me. If you enjoyed this story, please leave a Review[3]. I would really appreciate it.

---

1.   http://www.craigaprice.com/email-list.html

2. http://www.craigaprice.com/review-me.html

3. http://www.craigaprice.com/review-me.html

Prologue
Year 426 D.A.

A cold winter breeze blew through the window. Galedar shivered. He sat at a desk lit by the candlelight. A parchment lay in front of him, and a quill was in his hand. He needed help. People were after him. The Meldakar king knew he'd abandoned the army. Assassins were coming after him.

Galedar stood, rubbed his hands against his bare arms, and strode over to the window to close it. The red winter was rough this year. Normally, Galedar enjoyed the cold much more than the orange summers. However, he wanted warmth. It did not help that he was in hiding. He dared not make a fire, nor use the wood stove.

At his desk, he rubbed his hands together over the candlelight. It warmed his fingers a little, but it still wasn't enough. He looked down at his message. It wasn't perfect, but it would have to do. He needed help, and he didn't know who else to turn to. Brom was dead. A dragon had eaten him. Galedar didn't have many friends, or anyone he could trust.

A knock at the door startled him. He turned to look at his bed. The red dragon lay on his pillow, outstretched, on its back,

9

its belly exposed for all to see. And to top it all off, the creature was snoring.

Another knock startled the small dragon. The creature was growing fast. It had been only six weeks since the dragon hatched on the large island for him. He'd immediately begun repairing his ship to leave the island before a dragon ate him too. The baby dragon, however, refused to leave his side. Now, the little beast was as large as a sheepdog, and getting harder to hide.

"Noranda, hide," Galedar whispered.

The dragon huffed, smoke coming out of her nose. But she complied, crawling under the bed.

Galedar took a deep breath as he shuffled over to the door. He closed his eyes for a second, and then opened the door.

"Galedar, I knew I would find you here," an older man with a white mustache said.

Galedar froze. He gripped the door tight and tried to slam it on the man. This was his general in the war. The same general that he'd abandoned.

"Not so fast," the general snarled.

He pushed the door in, tossing Galedar to the ground.

"I can explain, Ilandor—"

Ilandor smacked Galedar across the face. "You are despicable. A coward. It gets too hard for you, and you run crying. What would your mother think?"

Galedar rubbed his face. "I don't want to be a part of any war."

"You are a traitor. I'm sure you know the king has placed your wanted posters all over the kingdom. I'm surprised you're still so close. What's wrong, Galedar? You didn't have enough coin to make it further than Laeraed?"

Galedar hung his head in shame.

"Get up," Ilandor yelled.

Galedar complied.

"I have a noose waiting on you outside. We're going to show all of Kaeldroga what Meldakar does to traitors." Ilandor spat on Galedar's face.

Galedar clenched his fists.

Ilandor laughed. "Don't even think about it. I have six guards posted outside. You won't make it far. I will give you some credit though, Galedar. At least you were smart enough to take the river south. I searched all the northern cities before thinking to come down here."

Galedar smiled. "I'm full of surprises."

Noranda growled. Ilandor looked to his feet, where he saw the small dragon. It bit his leg, its teeth tearing into his flesh. Ilandor yelled.

Galedar stepped forward, grabbing the sword from Ilandor's scabbard. Ilandor fell to his knees, fighting the dragon with his hands. Galedar slammed the general's weapon into the side of his neck. The general collapsed forward.

Six guards entered the room, weapons raised. Noranda snarled.

"What in the blazes is that?" one of the guards shouted.

"Attack, Noranda!"

The dragon leapt forward, claws slashing the face of the first guard. Galedar used the shock of seeing the dragon to his advantage as he stabbed his weapon through the chest of another. Noranda bit the throat of a third.

A few more blows of his sword, and vicious attacks of his dragon, and all six guards lay dead on the floor. Galedar piled them all together. He picked their pockets for coin and weapons before gathering everything into his bag and fleeing out the door. Before he left, though, he went back and grabbed the parchment he'd been working on. He really needed to find an ally. Galedar laid the candle on the desk, laying blank parchments on top of it.

When Galedar stepped outside, the flames began. People shouted in the streets. Ilandor had been right. People were outside, hoping for a hanging. He hated to disappoint them. They yelled and screamed at him, furious that he'd escaped the hanging. When Noranda rushed to his side, the shouts stopped. Everyone stared in horror at the dragon.

Galedar couldn't trust anyone, and Noranda was too big to hide anymore. He no longer tried. Everyone would know of her soon anyway. Now the rumors would spread.

Chapter 1
Year 511 D.A.

Zaviana watched the red sunrise as it broke into the horizon, casting a purple-and-orange glow into the sky. It was winter. She would miss the orange sun. Only the red sun showed its face during the winter. Its heat, somehow, was less than its orange twin's. Zaviana struggled, jerking her arms forward. Nothing. Her wrists hurt. She clenched her teeth. How did she go from being a prisoner to being a prisoner?

"You won't escape those chains, my love," Derkas? Said.

"If you really loved me, you wouldn't have me chained to a tree!" she snapped.

"Would you rather be chained to my dragon?" he asked.

Zaviana snarled. "I'd rather not be chained at all."

Derkas raised an eyebrow. "If I unchain you, do you promise to not run away?"

She scowled.

Derkas smiled. "I thought not."

"Why am I your prisoner?" she asked.

He tilted his head. "Would you rather be back with the emperor? In his prison?"

"No," she whispered.

"What did they do to you in there?"

She clenched her teeth. "Experiments."

"I'm sorry. I didn't know they captured you until it was too late."

"You didn't come for me. How can you claim to love me?"

"What can I do against the entire Dragonia Empire? I had to wait until I had enough leverage for a trade."

"A trade," Zaviana scoffed. "What could you possibly have had that they' were willing to trade me for?"

"The resistance."

Zaviana's eyes glowed. "The resistance? They're real then?"

"Yes, though they won't be for long."

"What do you mean?" she asked.

"I gave the emperor their hidden location for your freedom."

"My freedom? This isn't freedom. You exchanged their secret for my slavery. I am still a slave."

"What more do you want from me?" he asked. "I stopped that dragonrider from enslaving you when we first met. Now I've rescued you from the emperor."

"The emperor whom you let capture me."

"I did not let the emperor capture you. You ran away, straight into the arms of the empire."

"I ran away because you planned to hand over that man to the empire. I wanted to warn him."

"That man betrayed the Dragonia Empire. He fed information to the resistance. That is treason! He got what he deserved."

"No one deserves what the emperor did to him. No one."

"I didn't know ..."

"Of course you didn't know!" Zaviana snapped. "The emperor wasn't going to tell you he was going to skin him alive!"

"If I could go back ..." Derkas brushed his hand through his hair.

"You'd do the same thing over again," Zaviana said. "You mercenaries are all the same."

Derkas took two steps toward her. His face twisted in a snarl. He inhaled, loosening his expression, then brushed his hand against her cheek. It lingered for a moment before running through her hair, pressing it behind her left ear.

"I thought we had something," he whispered.

"You thought wrong." Zaviana shivered at his touch. "I thought you were different, someone I could trust. But I only fell for you because you saved me from that despicable dragonrider. You are no different."

He jerked his hand back, clenching his fist. His teeth ground together. He closed his eyes, exhaling slowly. When his eyes opened, he was fully relaxed once more.

"I am different."

Zaviana raised her brows. "Prove it."

"How can I prove this to you?"

"Let's warn the resistance."

His brow crinkled. "We can't."

"Why not?"

"Going against the Dragonia Empire is foolish. You should know that. Don't you remember what happened to your family when they defied the empire?"

Zaviana clenched her eyes shut, fighting back the tears that threatened to come. "Foolish it may be, but the empire is wrong. They were wrong for doing what they did, and they are wrong for everything they still do to threaten the people of Kaeldroga."

"It doesn't matter if what they do is moral or not. Who are you to judge? Even the creator hasn't stepped in to stop the Dragonia Empire. They are too strong. No one can stop them. Stop believing in the illusion that this so-called resistance will be able to stop them. They will be crushed like everyone who has tried. The best thing we can do is stay out of their way."

Zaviana glared at him. "You know as well as I that staying out of the way isn't good enough. Even if you don't defy them, if they believe you are standing in the way of someone who is ... they'll crush you."

Derkas grinned. "That's why I'm stepping out of the way."

"I refuse to hide," Zaviana said.

"And that is why you are still in chains. It is for your own good."

Chapter 2

Naveen trembled, her curly red locks of hair draping over her eyes. She couldn't believe what was happening. Her village burned. The Dragonia Empire claimed there were traitors in the village, sympathizers to the resistance. The three dragonriders were making a statement in the village.

The afternoon was quiet. All the villagers had given up the fight, though not many had attempted to defy the dragonriders in the first place—those who had were eaten alive by the dragons. Naveen had protested at first, when they took her friend, but after being backhanded by one of the riders and being told if she spoke another word she'd join her friend, she stood down. Naveen wondered if she'd made the right decision. She was alive, yes, but her friend stared at her from the gallows. Three others stood by nooses on the platform as well. They only had four nooses. There was a line of another eight people they'd rounded up, standing in line, waiting their turn to die.

Naveen's eyes welled up, and tears flowed down her face freely. Her best friend was about to die. And for what? Because the dragonriders believed her to be part of the resistance. Naveen knew better. Her friend had nothing to do with the resistance. But if Naveen said anything, she'd be hung as well.

Perhaps she should. Why accept the lie and let her friend die alone? Her teeth clenched. How could the Dragonia Empire do this? How could they make false accusations?

The lead dragonrider made sure all the nooses were secure around the four necks. He turned to face the crowd, a grin splitting his face in two.

"People of Anius. The Dragonia Empire has no sympathy for traitors. Let this be a lesson to you all. If you join the resistance, or feed them information, like these scum"—he gestured to the four behind him—"you will fall to the same fate."

"I am not a trait—" Yvanya, her friend, yelled.

The dragonrider snarled as he slapped her mid-sentence. "Lies!"

He turned to the executioner. "Pull the lever."

The man glanced to the crowd, fear clear in his expression, but shock as well. He knew the people accused were innocent. His pause was for only an instant before he jerked the lever. The trapdoors dropped beneath the four accused. Silence ensued. They struggled, but their words wouldn't escape with the nooses blocking their air passages.

Naveen looked away, wiping a tear from her face. She was a coward. She couldn't even face her friend, couldn't watch her die. Yvanya had looked at Naveen when the floor dropped from under her. Guilt formed a lump in her throat. She shivered.

"Next," the dragonrider called.

Naveen glanced back to the gallows. Four people hung, unmoving, each dangling like a broken flower hanging from its stem by a thread. Two women and two men. She knew all of them. They were all good people. Her eyes blurred as she tried to unfocus, to unsee the people she knew, the people she'd grown up with, dead. She inhaled, closing her eyes. When she exhaled, and her eyes opened, they betrayed her. The scene before her was crystal clear. Her eyes focused on Yvanya as they lowered her lifeless body from the noose. She looked calm, at peace. Naveen knew she was with the Creator now, walking in a land of paradise. She envied her friend. If the afterlife was indeed true, and it was indeed a paradise, it beat the horrid reality of the world Naveen was still stuck in. She should have had courage. She should have fought for her friend's innocence. Then they both could have died today. They could be in paradise together, or everlasting darkness. Whichever truth it was, it was better than this moment, this chaos. It was better than living a life under the rule of the Dragonia Empire.

The dragonriders finished hanging another eight people in the next hour. Naveen unfocused, barely noticing what was going on around her.

"Burn the traitors' homes," Naveen vaguely heard one of the dragonriders say.

She tuned it all out, refusing to accept the reality of the situation. It wasn't until someone nudged her that she snapped out of it.

"Naveen? Are you all right?"

Naveen shook her head. "Yeah. Sorry."

"I know it's hard on you. Hard to come to terms with the fact that Yvanya was a traitor. But you must move past—"

"Yvanya was not a traitor."

"Shh. Don't let the dragonriders hear you say that," Leland, the blacksmith, whispered.

Naveen stormed off, refusing to respond. She knew her friend. They'd been friends since little girls. If she was part of some secret resistance, Naveen would have known about it. Rumors had been spreading lately about this so-called resistance fighting the empire. She wondered if they stood a chance. Naveen hoped so. She wanted the Dragonia Empire to burn. Though, as she thought about it, why was the Dragonia Empire focused on killing innocents, claiming they were traitors? To spread fear? To make people scared to join the resistance? She pondered it as she walked back home. If they were trying to convince people to stay away from the resistance ... then it meant they were scared. Did they actually believe the resistance had a chance? Naveen knew nothing about the resistance, but now she desperately wanted to find them. She wanted to know if they were indeed strong enough to face the Dragonia Empire.

Chapter 3

Smoke filled the horizon, creating a swirl of smoke in the evening sunset. Zaviana had a little more freedom, but not much. Her hands were still bound, but they weren't as tight as days before. She could actually move around a little easier.

"Where are we going?" she asked.

Derkas glanced over to her. "Somewhere safe."

"Safe?" Zaviana scoffed. "There is nowhere safe from the Dragonia Empire."

"It's safer where they're not as active."

"And they're not active in the east? What does that mean? Is the resistance in the west?"

Derkas furrowed his brow.

"Don't give me that expression. I'm not an idiot. I watch the red sun. I know we're traveling toward its sunrise."

"East is safer," he responded.

"Why?" she asked.

He shook his head.

"Where are the resistance?"

"I'm not going to tell you."

"Why not?" she asked.

He sighed, brushing his hands through his hair. "Because you would try something foolish, like try to escape to warn them, or blab all over the next town about trying to save them. Like you, I am not foolish."

She wrinkled her nose. "So, this is what it comes to then? I'm to be your slave wife?"

He raised a brow. "Excuse me?"

"You don't trust me to let me loose. You don't trust me with where the resistance is, though Creator knows why you'd tell the Dragonia Empire and not me. Yet, you claim to love me, to want to be with me. I am not willing, but you have forced me to stay with you. I am your slave, but you want me to be with you. What is that? That is wrong."

"Tell me you don't have feelings for me."

She opened her mouth, but closed it. They'd spent over eight months together when she was free. Although, all the while, Derkas had been searching for the traitor, unbeknownst to her. Still, feelings formed. Even with his hardheaded mind-set, and chains to keep her from escaping, she'd be lying if she said there were no feelings at all.

"See? You can't even say it."

She let out a deep breath. "This is wrong, Derkas. Can't you see that? You can't keep me in chains forever. What about free will? Do you really want me to love you because I'm forced to? I would be a slave wife, and I would never be happy."

"You won't be in chains forever."

"I shouldn't be in chains now!"

"Those chains aren't to keep you locked to me. Can't you see, Zaviana? I've made a deal with the empire. Deals with the empire aren't easy to make. The last time I made a deal with the empire ... well, you remember. I turned in that traitor. And I received"—he gestured toward his dragon—"Chalce. She was just an egg at the time. But they never thought she'd hatch. Only red dragon eggs had hatched. They thought the blue ones were bad eggs. When they found out, they tried coming for me. They wanted to take the deal back. I refused, and no one who tried to take Chalce from me was successful."

"What does that have to do with me?" she asked.

He shook his head. "Can't you see, Zaviana? I gave up the resistance for you. If they march up to the resistance and find me there, the deal will be off, and they'll come for you. They finally backed off me over Chalce because I did win her fair and square. But if they feel betrayed, they won't rest until I'm dead and you're back in prison. If we warn them, the same thing will happen. If you escape, you will be 'fair game' to them. They gave you to me and I lost you, so they would take you back and I wouldn't have any more leverage to get you back."

Zaviana gulped. "I understand your reasoning. But I don't agree with it."

Derkas pressed his lips tightly together. "I'm sorry, Zaviana. But I must keep you locked up until the resistance is destroyed. Then, the emperor's blood-thirst will be quenched, and hopefully, if we're lucky, his attention will be far away from you. But right now ... I need to keep you safe."

"I won't run," she said.

He shook his head. "I wish I could believe you, really, I do."

She looked away from him, toward the smoke in the horizon. It had increased. A steady flow of thick black smoke flooded the sky.

"What is that smoke?" she asked.

Derkas glanced behind him and shrugged.

"That isn't from a campfire, is it?"

Derkas didn't move.

"Something is burning. It's the Dragonia Empire, isn't it?"

"I don't know," Derkas whispered.

"We should go see," Zaviana said.

"We shouldn't get involved."

"Why do you love me?"

"Excuse me?" he asked.

"Clearly you don't have the same morals as me. Clearly you don't care about people as much as I do. I want to make sure everyone's all right. Yet, you could care less. You are selfish, and I am selfless. Why, then, do you love me?"

He gritted his teeth. "I love you because you care ... because you make me care."

"Then care ... Let's go see what's going on with that smoke."

"Fine," he said through clenched teeth.

Chapter 4

Naveen shivered as she stepped out her door into the crisp winter air. The red sun peeked over the horizon, casting a pink glow in the sky in the east. It was cold already. The winter would only grow colder. A light layer of snow covered the ground. It had only just begun. Roosters crowed in the distance. Naveen would miss her village of Anius. However, she knew in her heart it was time to go.

There was nothing left for her in Anius. Her friend was gone, and her family had died years ago. It wasn't like she had a husband, nor did she particularly want one. Besides, no one would understand her secret. She'd have a harder time hiding it if she had a husband. They'd call her a witch and hang her. She was better off alone. Yvanya had known. But she had kept silent. Even during her prosecution and hanging, she hadn't said a word. She had protected Naveen, and what had Naveen done? Let her die? Not try to stop the hanging?

Naveen hung her head low, mentally kicking herself for all the things she'd failed to do to save her best friend. Though, what could she have truly done to save her? There were three dragonriders, which meant three hard-trained weapon masters, and three large dragons. She was nothing compared to them, even when considering her talent.

She brushed her auburn hair from her eyes as she strode to the center of the village. Everyone else was already awake and about. The dragonriders had left to who knows where. Probably to torment another village. Now, the villagers were left with the job of burying the dead.

Graves were being dug, and bodies were carried over to them. Naveen turned away when she saw her dead friend. Her eyes clenched shut. She couldn't face her dead friend today. She could barely face the other villagers. Something had to change. Naveen planned to leave.

When she turned around, she nearly ran into Leland. Naveen smiled at him. He'd always been kind to her.

"Good morning, Leland."

"Morning, Naveen. Are you leaving so soon?"

"I can't be here. This ... this is too much."

"I know. It seems ... unjust in a way."

"It is unjust. I knew all these people, and some I may not have known well, but others I did. They were not traitors."

"Keep your voice down. This is no time to stir the pot. The Dragonia Empire is looking for any reason for a hanging lately," he whispered.

"And why do you think that is?"

"I heard a rumor. Mind you, I don't know if it's true, but the rumor is the resistance won a battle," he whispered.

"They actually won a battle against the empire?" Naveen gasped.

"As I said, I don't know if it's true. And if it is, I doubt the empire was prepared for the battle. Might have caught them by surprise."

Her eyes gleamed. "Still, that is something."

"No, Naveen." He shook his head. "Don't you be getting any wild ideas."

Her eyebrows rose. "Too late."

Naveen strode past him, into the center of the crowd. She glanced around and climbed to the top of one of the large dirt piles. Everyone turned to face her as she cleared her throat.

"Today is a sad day. We have lost loved ones and we have lost friends. And if we're honest with ourselves, we know they were not the traitors they were made out to be."

"Naveen," Leland whispered to her through clenched teeth.

"No. I will not be silent. We knew these people. They were not traitors. They were friends. They were family. It seems clear to me the Dragonia Empire is attacking villages, hanging easy targets. All to scare us." She took a deep breath. "Why would they want to scare us?"

Everyone kept silent.

"Can't you see? They're scared. For the first time, the Dragonia Empire is scared. They are scared of the resistance. That's why they're trying to scare us from joining. Listen, I'm not a part of the resistance. I am not one they deem traitor. But, after seeing them slaughter innocents yesterday, I will not stay idly by for them to continuing killing whoever they choose. I am leaving. I will search for the resistance. I will join them. And somehow, we will stop the Dragonia Empire. Think about what side you're on."

A few people in the crowd nodded. Others looked at her with disgust or hatred. She didn't care. She'd said what she needed to say. Who took the message to heart was on them.

Naveen clutched her satchel as she climbed down the pile of dirt to a separating crowd. Leland stomped over to her.

"You shouldn't say such things. They may come for you next."

"I don't care." She scowled. "Let them. I'm not going to live the rest of my life in fear that they may want to murder me one day for doing nothing wrong. I'm not going to hide. I'm going to do something to try and stop them. I cannot let the empire get away with slaughtering innocents. Will you join me?"

He shook his head. "I will not."

She nodded in understanding. "Will you pray to the Creator for me?"

He nodded. "That, I can do. Honestly, I wish you the best. I hope you succeed."

She smiled. "Thank you, Leland."

Naveen turned around and made her way out of the village. She wasn't alone.

Chapter 5

Z aviana peered through the bushes at the village. It was small, as small as the village near the farm she'd grown up on. She glanced down at her hands. The chains were gone. Derkas put some trust in her. She wondered how long it would last. Still, he didn't leave her out of his sight. He stood behind her, watching over her as if she were a child.

She stepped forward, out of the bushes, and walked toward the village. Several buildings had been burned, but they were no longer on fire. Some were charred, while others were ashes. People in the village dragged bodies across the ground to a cemetery. Fresh graves were being dug.

No one even noticed when Zaviana and Derkas blended into the crowd. A gloom filled the air. People were distraught. Zaviana had a suspicion of what happened the night before. She didn't want her suspicions to be the truth, but once a woman climbed to the top of a dirt pile and began speaking, her fears were confirmed.

The people watched the speaker with interest. Some seemed angry, but many others were intrigued. Her speech was flawless. Zaviana had to give the woman credit. However, what she planned to do was dangerous. To seek the resistance was dangerous enough, but to openly seek them, that was signing your own death warrant. Zaviana knew if the resistance had spies in villages to recruit people, so would the empire.

Zaviana watched the crowd carefully, trying to locate who might be a spy for the empire. It was hard to focus, and Zaviana knew she didn't have too much time. She stepped back, closed her eyes, and focused. An image of a single flame in an expanse of darkness came to her mind. She focused on it, trying to get it to grow. Zaviana could feel the energy all around her, the life-source of every living creature. Every single being had energy inside of them. The energy came from food, water, and sunlight. She could steal their energy, a power she'd discovered when she was a child. An ability she had told no one about except her brother. Yet, the empire had discovered her ability after she escaped from the dragonrider who'd captured her from her farm. The one that Derkas had found, and killed, in order to free her. She was indebted to him for that, but when she was traveling with Derkas, she had accidentally let her power slip in order to save the two of them. It was that moment of desperation that the empire—or rather, one of its spies—had seen. That's when the empire came for her and stole her from Derkas.

She opened her eyes and began examining people. Their own energy was being used against them. Zaviana didn't use much of their energy, only a little bit from each person. She absorbed it, then channeled it out through her eyesight to see what she wanted to see. Colorful hues surrounded each person. The woman giving her speech on the mound of dirt was outlined in a glowing green, as were dozens more who surrounded her. Some were blue, indifferent about her speech. Others were yellow, angry with her words, but otherwise innocent.

Then, she saw it. After the woman finished her speech, she climbed off the mound and talked to a man. He was a burly man, round and tall, with thick shoulders. He wore a black leather apron and his face was covered in soot. From all appearances, he seemed to be a blacksmith. His aura was different than the rest. He was outlined in red.

"We need to go. This is not a good place for us to be," Derkas whispered.

She spun to face him. "No. There is a traitor here."

"Yeah ... that woman. The rest of her companions burned because of their beliefs. She'll be next."

"Everything she said is right. The empire must be stopped. If you'd get your head out of your behind, you'd see it too!"

"So, you're not talking about the resistance. Wait, are you using your power again?"

She turned away.

"Don't use your power. If someone finds out ... If they know what you can do ... Please. I don't want any more reason for the empire to come searching for you. We need to lay low for a while."

"I am done hiding."

His eyes widened. "Don't say that."

She slid through the crowd. Derkas stayed on her heels. The woman who gave the speech strode toward them. Zaviana froze as the woman walked in front of her, glancing to Zaviana for only an instant before continuing on her way out of the village. Zaviana watched as a hundred people from the village followed her. Some ran back into their homes to pack, others left with little more than the clothes on their backs. Zaviana could hardly believe her eyes. She hadn't expected so many to follow the woman. No wonder the empire was so scared of the resistance. People were finally fed up.

Zaviana almost lost the blacksmith. He slipped through the crowd, not looking back. He had acted like a friend to the woman, but Zaviana saw his aura. He was working directly for the empire. She saw him slip into a small cottage. He wasn't going back to work.

She stormed to the door of the cottage and focused again. The walls of the cottage became transparent as she focused. Her energy was fading. She'd have to siphon energy from the villagers again soon, or from plants. Inside, the man sat at a desk, a parchment in front of him and a quill in his hand. Zaviana clenched her teeth as she focused on him. Her vision zoomed in so she could make out his letter.

Village of Anius

Leland, Blacksmith

Naveen, a local seamstress, has taken hard the loss of her friend, one of the traitors of the empire. She has rallied many to her cause. They leave, south, searching for the resistance.

Zaviana's fingernails dug into her palms. She broke down the door, depleting the rest of her energy. The door glowed green for an instant as it shattered inward. Derkas cursed behind her. She didn't care. The man jumped from his desk, a dagger unsheathed from his boot.

"Who are you?" he asked.

"The question is … what are you doing?"

"Nothing. I'm tired after last night's events." He stepped in front of his desk, his body hiding the parchment.

"You are going to betray that woman. You've probably known her all her life, and you're going to betray her. Why?"

"I don't know wha—"

Derkas stepped next to her, a scimitar in his hand.

"What are you going to do?"

"Give me the parchment."

He shook his head. "No."

Zaviana's teeth clenched. She focused her power again, but she didn't have enough energy. The blacksmith was full of energy. Her hands quivered as she sucked energy from him to use. His entire body shook. Wrinkles formed on his face.

"What are you doing to me?" he asked in a shaky voice.

"Why are you betraying her?" she repeated.

"She's a traitor!" he yelled. "She doesn't deserve life. The emperor won't tolerate traitors."

"So you work directly for the emperor?"

"I ... I ..."

Her fingernails dug so far into her palms that her hands began to bleed. She lost control of her power. The blacksmith cried out as the rest of his life source left him. He shriveled as he took his last breath, falling to the floor. She didn't stop. His body deteriorated until all his flesh was gone. Derkas touched her shoulder. She jerked, but released her mental hold. Her hands relaxed as she spun to face the mercenary.

"Are you all right?" he asked.

She glanced to the blacksmith crumbled on the ground. He was no longer flesh. All that remained were his bones inside loose clothing. She hadn't known she could do that. No wonder the emperor had wanted her so much. She needed to control her anger.

"Sorry. I lost control."

"I can see that. I hope you never get that mad at me."

She smirked. "Don't give me a reason to."

"So, you're really serious about helping this resistance?"

She walked over to the desk, grabbed the parchment, held it over the candle on the desk, then dropped it back on the desk. It burned. Several other parchments on the desk caught fire. Zaviana didn't care. She walked toward the shattered door of the cottage.

She glanced back to Derkas and smiled. "Yes. You're not planning on getting in my way, are you?"

He shook his head.

Chapter 6

Naveen rubbed her hands against her arms. She wore thick cotton to protect her from the winter winds, but it was growing colder with each passing day. It wasn't going to get any better as they traveled south.

They entered the next village south. Anaiah seemed to be in as much disarray as her village. Smoke rose from several burnt buildings. Villagers worked together to bring dead men and women to a graveyard. Naveen saw the bruised necks. Her eyes clenched shut. They'd had their friends and family hung as well.

She ran forward. The villagers looked at her suspiciously. Her hundred companions lingered behind her. She stood among the villagers at the cemetery where new graves were being dug.

"What happened here?" she asked.

No one responded. Only a few of the diggers glanced her way. The gloom of the event had everyone silent.

"Answer me! Did the Dragonia Empire do this to you?"

Still, no one responded.

"Listen, they came to our village too. They killed innocent people, claiming they were part of a resistance. They are trying to scare you away from joining. If you want to fight against the injustices of the Dragonia Empire ... follow me."

"Follow you where?" a woman finally asked.

"I am going to search for the resistance," Naveen said with confidence.

"Traitor," a man growled.

Naveen turned to face him. "Excuse me?"

"It's because of people like you that our friends and family are dead."

"I had nothing to do with your family's death. The Dragonia Empire did."

"They killed them because of traitors like you trying to give them a false sense of hope with lies of the resistance. What makes you think they'll be any better? Even if they do win, which they won't, they'll just rule the same as any other."

"I don't believe that."

"Traitor," he spat.

"Look, I am not with the resistance. My friends and family were murdered by the Dragonia Empire as well. That was when I decided that I can no longer stand by and let them do this to innocent people."

"Get out of here with your false hope," the man said.

Naveen scanned her surroundings. She could tell her speech wasn't as effective as in her village. Most of the villagers were too scared or angry to join her. She sighed and turned around.

Naveen didn't leave the village yet. She lingered, watching the people bury their loved ones. A tear fell down her face at the injustice of it all.

"Excuse me, miss?"

She glanced to her side. A young man with a brown beard and curly hair stood by her side, facing her.

"Yes?" she asked.

"Are you really searching for the resistance?"

"I am."

"I want to join you."

She raised an eyebrow.

He took a deep breath. "My father was the shoemaker in this village. Those dragonriders hung him because he made shoes for villagers who were suspected of being with the resistance."

"That's terrible."

He nodded. "I can't stay here. I can't do nothing. I ... I ..." He wiped away a tear. "I want to avenge him."

"Have you ever wielded a weapon?"

He frowned. "No."

"You said your father was a shoemaker. Were you his apprentice?"

"Yes, miss."

"What is your name?" she asked.

"Cederic."

Naveen smiled at him. "We could use a shoemaker on our journey."

He grinned. "Let me gather my supplies."

She noticed a few others coming over to her, supplies in hand. A twinkle came to her eye as she smiled at them and welcomed them to her party. It wasn't as many as had followed her from her village, but it was still comforting to have more allies. She made a quick head count to find another twenty, including the shoemaker, had joined her.

Once everyone was together, she made ready to leave. Someone bumped into her. Naveen spun around, seeing a young brown-skinned woman with long black hair reaching for her. She backed away. A tall man grabbed the woman, dragging her away.

"I'm sorry," he said.

"I must tell her," the woman demanded.

"Not now," he whispered to her.

Naveen started to go after her, but they were too fast, and she lost track of them as they disappeared into the crowd.

"Must tell me what?" Naveen whispered.

"Traitors, traitors, traitors!" the crowd chanted.

Naveen's eyes widened. Villagers stomped toward her with pitchforks and torches. She backed away a few steps as Cederic ran to her side.

"Hang her," someone from the crowd yelled.

"Run," Cederic called.

Naveen turned on her heel and sprinted out of the city. The twenty newcomers joined her along with the hundred from her village.

Chapter 7

Zaviana looked around Anaiah, mouth agape and eyes wide. This was the second village in a row where the Dragonia Empire had cast judgment on innocent villagers. It was like deja vu. Bodies were dragged off the gallows and buried in the cemetery. Zaviana noticed a difference though. Whereas the last village had faces of anger or determination after the event, these faces were grim, sad, and lost. They had no hope.

Derkas walked by her side. They stopped as they watched the same scene play out before them. Dead villagers were carried to the cemetery and dropped into graves.

Zaviana turned to Derkas. "Look me in the eyes and tell me what the Dragonia Empire is doing is right."

He turned away from her.

"Will you help me?"

"Help you do what?"

"Warn the resistance? Fight against the tyranny of the empire?"

"Whoa ... wait. Zaviana, what you're saying is treason."

"What I'm saying is the right thing to do."

"No. I will not allow you to put yourself in danger."

She raised an eyebrow at him. A woman began speaking in the crowd. Zaviana turned around to notice the same woman from the last village. Her speech was similar, trying to convince the villagers to follow her and find the resistance. This time, however, the crowd wasn't as well received.

Only a few people talked to her and followed her after her speech. Everyone else didn't look impressed. Zaviana jerked away from Derkas, escaping his clutches, and she dashed over to the woman. She needed to tell her, to warn her about the empire's plans, and to tell her where the resistance was, as soon as she learned herself.

Zaviana reached her, but was grabbed by Derkas from behind. Her grip slipped and she was pulled away. Her body tightened and she used all her strength to try and tear away from Derkas. He was too strong.

"I have to tell her," she said.

"I'm sorry," Derkas said to the woman as he pulled Zaviana away.

Zaviana tried to focus, tried to use the elements around her to give her power, but she couldn't concentrate. She wasn't good at using her magic under pressure.

He slammed her on the ground outside of the village. The dragon approached and sniffed her, trying to rub her snout against Zaviana.

"No, Chalce. Don't coddle her!" He turned around to face Zaviana. "Don't you understand? You'll be the death of us by doing things like this. Openly defying the empire is signing your own death sentence. That's exactly what that woman is doing. Watch, she won't last long. Soon, dragonriders will catch her and make an example of her."

"You can stop it," Zaviana said.

"Excuse me?" Derkas asked.

"You can prevent her from being killed by the empire."

He snarled, turning away from her.

"All you have to do is show her the way to the resistance. Even if you don't join, you can save her, and let her fate be with the resistance."

"Her fate with the resistance would be little better than at the hands of the empire."

"But," Zaviana said, "it would be better."

Derkas didn't say a word as he took out the cuffs and chained her to a tree. She tried to fight against him, tried to summon her magic, but could do nothing.

"You will stay with me from now on, and if we have to stay out of the villages, so be it."

The dragon inched its nose closer to Zaviana and growled.

Zaviana hung her head in defeat.

Chapter 8

Naveen clutched her blankets tighter as she huddled around the fire. Here she was, hiding from the empire by a fire in the snow. The long winter was the worst time to try to hide. It was too bloody cold. White breath fluttered from her mouth as she rubbed her hands together. A few inches of snow had fallen the night before. At least it wasn't full-on winter yet. It was only going to get worse the further south they traveled.

The shoemaker, Cederic, shuffled over to Naveen. He didn't appear to be cold in the slightest. Naveen glared at him.

"Are you cold, miss?" he asked her.

"It's Naveen. Don't call me miss."

"Sorry ... Naveen."

"Yes ... I'm a bit cold. I'm not used to the south. I'm from the north. It doesn't get as cold up there."

"Are your feet cold?" he asked.

She smiled. "No. Thank you for the new shoes."

He returned her smile. "So where are we headed? Where is the resistance?"

Naveen glanced around to make sure no one else was close enough to overhear. "I don't know where the resistance is."

His eyes bulged. "You don't know?"

She shook her head.

"Where are we leading all these people?"

"I'm traveling village to village, trying to convince people to join the resistance. Hopefully, the resistance will have someone in one of these villages."

"You're putting all your faith in stumbling across someone who knows where the resistance is?"

She took a deep breath. "I don't know what else to do. I can't explain it, but I've always had this extra sense of knowing what was right. I know when something is a bad idea or a good idea. I felt an overwhelming cold deep inside when the dragonriders first arrived in my village. I told my friends about it, but no one believed me until it was too late. Now, I have an overwhelming sense of warmth deep inside as we travel south."

"You're basing all of this off your sense? You're leading all of us south, into the heart of winter." Cederic exhaled, a white cloud of breath flooding from his mouth. "What if you're wrong?"

Naveen rubbed her hands together. "That is my biggest fear. So far, my sense has never been wrong. But my fear is ... what if I've just imagined this extra sense ... what if it's all in my head? What if I'm wrong this time?"

Cederic gulped. "I'm sure everything will be all right."

"Don't say anything, all right?" Naveen asked. "I still have the feeling we're going the right way. Let's make it to the next village first before we decide the future of our path."

He nodded.

Tobias walked over to them. He was a chef who had joined them from the last village. His hands were bare and held two carving knives, which he slid together.

"The people are getting hungry. I'm getting antsy. We need to find food to cook."

Naveen glanced around the white-covered terrain. She was afraid of that. They hadn't brought enough food for the journey. And since winter had begun, it wouldn't be easy to find animals to hunt.

"It's hard to find food in the winter. Just find me some squirrels and I can create a stew."

"Squirrels?"

"Yeah ... tree rats."

Her face scrunched up. "Rats?"

"Or go see if you can find something larger. Just find something. People are starting to get hungry. Hungry people question motives. If you don't want problems on this journey, you need to keep everyone's belly full."

Another man stepped next to the chef. He didn't look to be from her village, so Naveen assumed he was from the last one. A bow was strapped across his shoulder and a quiver of arrows hung on his back.

"I'm a hunter and a tracker. I could search for food."

Naveen nodded. "I'll come with you. I don't think any of us should travel alone. What is your name?"

"All right. My name is Lesharo."

"Lesharo. Perhaps you could teach me some of your tracking skills."

He smiled at her. "I would be happy to."

She turned to Cederic. "Please keep an eye on everyone here, and help them if you can."

"Yes, milady."

Naveen and Lesharo grabbed a few weapons from their packs and strode out of the camp. She wasn't a skilled tracker, but she had hunted before and wasn't completely clueless. However, it also had a lot to do with her extra sense. She might not notice the tracks or the scents, but when she focused on her goal, an internal tugging led her. Naveen felt the dagger at her belt and the loaded crossbow on her back.

"Do you really think the resistance has a chance?" the hunter asked.

Naveen turned her head to glance at him. They were well away from their camp now. Even though he was the tracker, she found herself leading him.

"Yes. I do. I heard that they won a battle in the southwest."

He frowned. "I heard the same thing. But that can't be true, can it?"

Her eyebrows rose. "I don't see how it can't. This didn't happen that long ago, and right after, the empire is sending out dragonriders to all the villages to scare them into not joining the resistance. Why would they do that if they won that battle?"

His nose scrunched back and forth. "Hmm ... you're right."

Naveen stopped. She gestured to Lesharo to be silent. He paused, looking at her quizzically, but complied. She closed her eyes and reached out with her extra sense. A grin split her face. She saw an elk in her mind.

"This way," she whispered.

"What is it?"

She put her finger over her mouth and gestured him to follow. He raised his eyebrows but continued to follow her lead. They slid through a patch of trees to a field of head-tall grass.

Naveen crept closer, brushing the tall grass out of the way. An elk stood less than a hundred feet away. It leaned down eating grass.

Lesharo's face furrowed as he considered Naveen. She pointed to his bow. He shook his head and nocked an arrow. Judging the distance and slight breeze, he took aim and loosed. The arrow struck the elk in the chest, and it shrieked before galloping off. Lesharo stood, ready to track the animal as it bled.

The elk dashed away into the woods. Lesharo and Naveen followed. Naveen could sense which way the animal went, but she let the huntsman lead. He followed swiftly, until they could no longer see the elk, then he inspected the trail. From stomped grass to broken sticks and droplets of fresh blood, he followed a narrow path in the direction the elk took.

Naveen followed him for a while, then she abruptly stopped. Her vision went black and she felt dizzy. She shivered, fear consuming her. Something wasn't right.

"Lesharo!" she called.

The hunter stopped, turned around, and saw her distress. He paused for an instant before rushing back to her.

"Are you all right?" he asked.

"Something is wrong," she said.

He held out his hand to her, as if to help her stand.

"Not with me," she said. "There is danger ahead."

He tilted his head. "How do you know?"

"I can sense it."

His brows furrowed.

"It's hard to explain. I've always been able to sense things. That's how I found the elk. It's how I know something is wrong ahead of us."

"Well, if there's danger this close to our camp, shouldn't we find out what it is?" he asked.

Naveen gulped. "Yes."

He motioned for her to follow him. He stepped forward cautiously, tiptoeing with each step. Naveen followed him close behind. They crept deeper into the forest until Lesharo abruptly stopped. Naveen leaned around him to see what he saw.

The elk lay dead on the ground next to a fire. A large red dragon took bites out of the flesh as a man roasted a chunk of the meat over a fire.

"Shouldn't we search for whoever was hunting this elk?" a clean-shaven man asked.

Naveen's eyes shifted, and she noticed a second dragon. Her body tensed. There were two dragonriders. Fear overcame her. Her emotions quickly turned to hate as she watched the two men—the same two dragonriders who had come to her village and murdered her friend. She clenched her teeth.

"Probably just some villagers," the man roasting elk by the fire said. He had a thick red beard. "Don't worry about them. We'll deal with the village to the south in the morning. I want a safe night's sleep for once. Sooner or later, one of these villagers is going to snap and try something on us."

The clean-shaven man laughed. "Let them try."

"I know they won't be successful. But we're hanging their friends and family. Someone is bound to snap."

"Meh, who needs a bunch of traitors in the empire anyway?"

"I hope they're all traitors," the red-bearded man by the fire whispered.

"What's that?"

"I just find it strange that we're sent on a killing rampage just after the battle in the west."

"It's not strange. The emperor is showing the people what happens to traitors. The last thing he wants is more foolish people joining the resistance."

Naveen tapped Lesharo's shoulder. She dared not speak, not knowing how well the dragonriders could hear, or the dragons for that matter. He pried his eyes away from the dragonriders to look at her. She motioned for them to leave. He nodded.

They barely made it ten steps before Naveen stepped on a branch. It snapped. The two dragonriders stopped talking. A low growl filled the silence.

Lesharo and Naveen looked at each other with wide eyes. They ran. Naveen didn't turn around, didn't try to keep Lesharo in sight, all she did was run. Her senses took over her navigation as she twisted and turned through trees until finding a bank at the bottom of a tree overhanging a small cliff. She dropped to the ground and found a hole paralleling the ground next to the roots of the tree. She didn't want to think about what might live inside. Naveen took a deep breath, put her feet into the hole, and pushed her body inside as far as it would go. Once secure, she lay motionless. Her senses relaxed.

She heard commotion near her and held her breath. A man grunted.

"Now, now," she heard the voice of one of the dragonriders. "What are you doing way out here in the forest by yourself?"

"Hunting," Lesharo muttered.

"Hunting ... alone? Do you often travel the forests by yourself?"

"I enjoy hunting alone."

"Where's the rest of your party?"

"I am alone."

"I don't buy it, do you?" asked Red-beard.

"Nope," the clean-shaven man said.

"The question is ... what do we do with him?"

"Hmm ... well, our dragons are hungry. Or, we could hang him in the next village as a lesson not to disobey the Dragonia Empire."

"Why is he this far away from a village in the winter?"

The clean-shaven dragonrider raised his eyebrows. "Good question. He should already have a reserve of food for the winter."

"I believe we may have caught our first resistance scum."

A short silence followed.

"I believe you may be right. Tell me, hunter, are you with the resistance?" Red-beard asked.

"No. I am loyal to the empire."

"Do you believe him?" Red-beard asked.

"Not even a little."

"What do you think we should do?"

"Take him back to the general ... after searching for his companions," the clean-shaven man said.

"I am alone."

A smack and a thud as someone collapsed to the ground followed. Naveen shivered, but remained silent. She hated that Lesharo had been captured, but she couldn't let herself be captured as well. A stick broke under her arm as she tensed.

"What was that?" one of the dragonriders asked.

Naveen's entire body became rigid. She held her breath as she heard footsteps approach. The air surrounding her warmed as she heard a strong sniff. Dead leaves all over the ground swirled up in front of her in a tornado. Sweat covered her face. After several long seconds, she heard footsteps leaving.

She remained still for several minutes until she heard flapping wings disappearing into the distance. Her body collapsed onto the ground and she let out a long breath.

Chapter 9

Zaviana scraped the ground with a stick. Her mind jumped all over the place. She needed to get away from Derkas, to help the resistance, to help the woman trying to find them. She needed to know where the resistance was. Most of all, she wanted a bath. She'd spent years as a slave in the Dragonia Empire, and now weeks traveling with the mercenary. All the while, she hadn't bathed but a few times, and not once during their travels.

"Can I have a bath?" she asked.

Derkas craned his head away from the fire to stare at her. His brows furrowed, and his bottom lip slid to the side.

"A bath?"

"Yes."

"We're stuck out in the wilderness, trying to stay hidden from the Dragonia Empire ... and the foolish people of the resistance ... and you want a bath?"

Her nose wrinkled. "Yes."

"Look, we don't have time right now for you to be a proper lady."

"Proper lady? How would I ever feel like a proper lady? I'm chained to a flaming tree!"

"I'm sorry I have to do that, but I can't trust you."

"Look, a bath has nothing to do with me being a proper lady. I've been stuck in the wilderness for weeks now. Before you purchased me, I was with the Dragonia Empire for years. They hardly let me bathe either. I'm filthy, and I haven't had an actual bath in months. All I want is to feel clean for once."

"This is not the time. A war is about to begin."

"What war? The war you pushed? It's not going to be a war, it's going to be a slaughter!"

"You're right. It is. That's why there's no need to support the resistance. They won't be here much longer. We'll see them crumble."

"Why does the flaming war matter anyway? You said you brought me far away from the empire to safety."

Derkas paused, his eyes flicking from side to side.

Zaviana's eyes widened. "You didn't take me away from the war, did you?" She shook her head. "Of course you didn't. You can't stay out of it; you want to see the destruction firsthand."

Derkas was silent.

"But why would you want that? As a mercenary, you could aid whoever is winning, or offer help to the victor. But that would require doing another job, and you're supposed to be protecting me. So, either you want to know the outcome firsthand, or you want to be close enough for me to witness it."

He remained silent.

"You're hoping the resistance falls. That way you can show me how hopeless it is to fight the empire. That's it, isn't it? With the resistance crumbled, you're hoping I'll crawl into your arms and ask you to protect me."

"The resistance will fall," he said.

"Perhaps, but I can still hope. The Dragonia Empire needs to fall."

"They won't. They have dragons."

"So do you." Zaviana raised an eyebrow.

"I have one dragon. They have hundreds."

"The resistance has opposed the empire for a long time. Don't you think they've developed a way to combat dragons by now?"

"One or two, maybe ... but a hundred? They don't stand a chance."

"So, where are they?"

He raised an eyebrow.

"The resistance. Where are they?"

Derkas remained silent.

"We're just outside the last village south. There are no villages south of Whistauf, are there? I believe there once were, but they were destroyed in the dragon war that brought the empire to power. There are no forests around here. The resistance won't be in the open. They'd have to have a refuge away from civilization." She gasped. "They're in the mountains, aren't they?"

Derkas glanced away.

Zaviana smiled.

"I'm going to find dinner," Derkas said.

"If you're so intent on keeping me safe, why are you brining me to the heart of battle?"

"The safest place is right under their nose. They'll never suspect you being there, or me."

"Close enough to smell the blood," she whispered. "Does that make you feel good?"

"Excuse me?"

"Knowing you condemned a bunch of innocents to their death?"

Derkas gritted his teeth. "They are not innocent. They are traitors, and they deserve what's coming to them."

"No one deserves that," she whispered.

Derkas grabbed some supplies. "Stay here, I'm going to fetch dinner."

She raised her hands into the air, showing him the shackles. "You don't leave me much of a choice."

He shrugged before disappearing into the trees.

Zaviana scowled. The dragon walked over to her and lay on the ground behind her. Zaviana took a deep breath, sat, and leaned her head against the side of the dragon.

"I wish we could convince Derkas to do the right thing."

The blue dragon, whose head rested on her paws, lifted her head to look at Zaviana.

Zaviana stroked the dragon's muzzle, feeling the soft scales of the dragon's face.

"I just wish he would see how evil the Dragonia Empire is, how corrupt they are. No one should govern people with fear, with tyranny. I just want peace in the land, and that won't come with the Dragonia Empire. If there's some way we can make the resistance win, I believe everything would get better."

The dragon rumbled, as if it were purring. It leaned closer to Zaviana, nuzzling against her leg. She giggled, moving her hand behind the dragon's ear. Zaviana scratched hard behind the creature's ear. The rumble increased and its foot began to tap on the ground. Zaviana laughed, imagining the dragon as a giant dog. Its mouth opened, and a cool blue mist trailed out. It covered several sticks on the ground, turning them a light blue. Zaviana knelt on the ground and touched one of the sticks. Her hand recoiled, burning from cold at the touch. She kicked the sticks and watched as they shattered into millions of pieces. Zaviana looked away from the crumbled sticks as an idea formed in her mind. She continued to pet the dragon, soothing the creature into a slumber. Once the dragon was asleep, she leaned her head against its belly and closed her eyes.

A little while later, Derkas returned to the camp carrying a handful of fish. A grin split his face as he tossed them by the fire.

Zaviana yawned. "Are those the largest fish you could find?"

She frowned at the pile of small fish.

Derkas dropped a large bag on the ground. A large silver fish slid out. He whistled faintly, startling the dragon awake. Derkas smiled at her, his expression warming with love.

Sometimes I wish he looked at me that way. Zaviana's face twisted. What am I thinking, no, I don't wish that. I don't need to feel for this scoundrel. He'd have the whole resistance collapse because he's too scared to do anything about it.

Derkas tossed the fish toward the dragon, who caught it in its mouth. It swallowed it whole, then licked its chomps.

Zaviana recoiled, not at the act of the dragon eating the fish, but at the smell that began to come from the creature's mouth.

Derkas cooked the fish, and when they were done, the two of them ate a silent dinner.

"Are you going to lie on Chalce all night?"

"I think I will," Zaviana said. "She's comfy."

Derkas frowned. He checked that her chains were secure, then bundled up in blankets and lay down next to the fire.

Zaviana watched him, listening closely for his breathing. When his breathing came in slow steady inhalations and exhalations, she waited for another ten minutes before beginning her plan. She leaned forward, careful to not wake the dragon. Zaviana reached over and began scratching Chalce behind the ear. The dragon was still asleep, but a rumble began inside of its throat. Zaviana carefully moved her other hand above the dragon's snout, holding the chain steady in front of its mouth. She increased her scratching behind the dragon's ear. The creature shifted in its sleep, but still didn't awake. Its mouth opened and a blue mist flooded out, encasing her chains. She watched with wide eyes as her chains turned from gray to blue. Zaviana carefully removed her hand from behind the dragon's ear and lay against the dragon's belly once more. She laid her chains on the ground next to her and slammed her foot on the frozen links. They shattered with a crunch that echoed through the camp. She slid the broken chains under her legs and closed her eyes.

She waited for several minutes, listening to the breathing of the dragon and Derkas. Neither breathed irregularly. She opened her eyes and noticed they were both in the same spots. Her eyebrows raised, her eyes smiling, she stood, took one last look at the dragon and the human, and carefully made her way out of the camp.

Chapter 10

Naveen walked into the camp. It was abandoned. She couldn't even tell her companions had stayed there. The fire pit had been buried, and all tracks were erased. Naveen wasn't an expert tracker, but she couldn't find footprints anywhere, or anything that would have implied a party of people had stayed there a few days prior.

She glanced around one more time. Naveen was sure it was the spot. Her extra sense had led her back. Naveen's ability had never led her astray.

They were gone.

Naveen was alone.

She took a deep breath, sat on a log, and reached out with her senses. The blackness under her eyelids transformed into a red glass lens as she viewed the forest in her mind. She reached out, searching the forest, like she was running in it herself. Even with her senses stretched, she still could not sense or see any trace of anyone.

Something touched her shoulder. The red lens disappeared. She opened her eyes, rolled forward, reached for an arrow in her quill, and brought it in front of her like a weapon.

A man stood behind the log where she had sat. He had a weapon on his belt, but he didn't reach for it. His hands were spread apart, palms up as he watched her.

Naveen's hands quivered, ready to spring. She relaxed slightly and focused on the man. Naveen recognized him. He was from the first village, one of the men who followed her.

"Kadier?" she asked.

He nodded.

"Where is everyone?"

"When you left to search for food, Cederic posted guards all around the camp. Good thing too, because one of them spotted a dragon in the sky. It's lucky he could see so well in the dark."

"Is everyone safe?" Naveen asked.

He smiled reassuringly. "Yes, we all hid in a cave west of here."

"A cave?"

"Yes, another lucky find. From the same man who saw the dragon, actually."

Naveen bit her lip. "Interesting. I would like to talk to this man."

Kadier smiled. "Let's head to the cave. I believe we all have a few questions for him. He's also the one who told me to come out here and find you ... as if he knew you were going to be here at this exact moment."

Naveen furrowed her brow.

NAVEEN WAS RELIEVED to see everyone inside the cave. Besides the hunter who was captured with her, no one else had been harmed. Kadier introduced her to the young man who'd sensed the danger. She walked with him away from the others so they could have a private conversation.

"I heard you had a feeling where I was."

He nodded.

"And that danger was coming."

He nodded again.

"What is your name?" she asked.

"Fraeyn."

"It's nice to meet you. You're young."

"Fourteen, ma'am."

"Ma'am? Well, I see your parents raised you well. Where are they?"

His eyes fell. He took a deep breath as he stared at his feet. "They were hung, ma'am."

Naveen nodded. She had expected as much. "And this ability of yours ... how long have you known about it?"

He shrugged. "All my life. My parents told me to keep it secret. That people wouldn't understand."

"They were right. My parents told me the same thing."

He looked up, meeting her eyes. "You ..."

She nodded. "Yes, I can sense things as well. Until I met you, I thought I was the only one."

"What is it? This ability we have ... is it magic?"

Naveen laughed. "I don't know, Fraeyn. Magic has always been a fairy tale. It's something old men say around a campfire. I don't think it's real. It seems we have an extra sense. Instead of sight, smell, hearing, touch, and taste, we also have a danger sense or a sense of where someone is. Perhaps it's a directional sense."

Fraeyn frowned. "Are you sure it can't be magic? I heard a legend that dragons were a fairy tale as well ... and now they've been used by the Dragonia Empire for over a hundred years to establish a tyrannical government."

Naveen bit her lip. "Whatever it is, I'm sure we haven't unlocked its full potential."

"How do we do that?" he asked.

"I don't know. We'll have to explore that together. Tell no one. I think it'd be best if we keep this our secret for now."

He nodded his understanding.

Chapter 11

Stars filled the night sky all around Zaviana. She lay alone on the grass, staring up at them. They were always much brighter in the winter when they only saw the red sun. Zaviana had eluded Derkas for one day, but she didn't know how much longer she'd be able to avoid him. She knew she was close to Whistauf and her last destination before fleeing to the mountains. Zaviana hoped she'd be able to make it in time. Derkas wasn't slow; she remembered that. A part of her, a part she hadn't known' existed, missed him—his touch, his concern for her, and his watchful eye. She didn't know what was wrong with her. Zaviana had every right to hate him. He'd kidnapped her, taken her against her will. Yes, he did it out of concern for her ... and that was sweet ... but she was missing the point. He was a scoundrel, a mercenary. Derkas couldn't possibly care about her that much. He cared about money. She couldn't count on him. Yet, she couldn't get him out of her head.

She sighed, closing her eyes. Zaviana needed rest. Perhaps a night or two away from him, and she'd get back to normal.

As soon as she closed her eyes, a shiver ran down her body. She saw Derkas' dragon in her mind as it descended near her, blowing ice all around her. Her eyes snapped open. She focused her senses. Flapping wings echoed in her ears. She jumped to her feet and concentrated, wrapping her tunic tighter around her. Zaviana closed her eyes, imagining herself encased in mirrored glass. Energy around her flickered, the air grew colder, and the grass below the snow died. She raised her hand and gazed right through it. She could see the light bending where her hand should be, like looking through transparent glass as it bent the light. It would have to do. Zaviana held onto the power as she ran. She wouldn't be able to delay another night. Zaviana needed to reach Whistauf tonight.

She didn't look behind her as she ran. It took another two hours before she reached Whistauf. She slowed. Her mind exhausted, her illusion keeping her invisible faded. She looked down at her brown hands and frowned. Zaviana rubbed them together, trying to warm them. She spun around, finally looking behind her, and gasped. Footprints trailed behind her. She smacked her forehead for her foolishness. All she did was waste her power, her energy. Derkas may not have seen her, but her footprints led straight to Whistauf. She backed away, shivering.

Something bumped into her. Zaviana turned around, raising her hands up in attack position. Her eye twitched as her vision came into focus. It was the woman from the villages, the one who'd tried to unite the villagers to fight against the empire.

The woman's forehead creased as she studied Zaviana. "Do I know you? You look familiar."

"I tried to talk to you ... a few villages ago, but I was pulled away," Zaviana responded carefully.

"That's right. Your husband pulled you away."

Zaviana scoffed. "He wishes. He is not my husband. He was my captor."

The woman raised an eyebrow. "Your captor?"

Zaviana held her hand out. "Zaviana."

The woman grabbed Zaviana's hand carefully. "Naveen."

A jolt of electricity traveled between them through their hands. They tensed, stared each other in the eyes for a second, then released hands.

"Zaviana? What were you trying to tell me in the village?"

"You are in danger. The resistance is in danger."

Naveen raised an eyebrow. "I'm not with the resistance."

Zaviana glanced from side to side. She noticed the small party of people accompanying Naveen. Two men and a woman. Each wore thick leathers to protect them from the cold.

"You mean you're not with them yet. I happen to know where they are."

Naveen's eyebrows quirked. "You do, do you?"

"Yes, but they won't be safe for long. We need to reach them before it's too late."

"What are you talking about?" Naveen asked.

"The empire is coming. They know where the resistance is hiding. We need to warn them."

"How can I trust you?"

"You can't." Zaviana sighed. "But do you have a choice?"

Naveen's nose wrinkled. "Where are they?"

"East ... in the mountains."

Naveen's brow furrowed. "East? How far north or south?"

Zaviana shook her head. "Directly east. We must hurry. I don't know when Derkas will catch up with me."

"Who?"

Zaviana sighed. "Derkas. The man who wouldn't let me talk to you. He's a mercenary, and the one who found the resistance and told the empire where they are. He held me prisoner, but I escaped two nights ago. He will be looking for me."

"I suppose you're right. I have no choice. The rest of my allies are outside of the village. We'll have to stop there to collect them."

Zaviana nodded. "Let's hurry."

Chapter 12

Three hundred people trekked up the mountain. Naveen and Zaviana led them. They talked a little during the journey, but most of all, they tried to keep warm. Snow already covered the ground all throughout the south, but the mountains were even worse. Instead of mere inches of snow, they had feet of snow to tread through. They made it between the two mountains to find many more mountains blocking their way.

"Where exactly is this place?" Naveen asked.

Zaviana closed her eyes. "Someone approaches."

Naveen shivered, her senses starting to throb in her mind. She furrowed her brow at Zaviana. Was she able to use an extra sense as well? Naveen opened her mouth to ask, but closed it when a small force of warriors appeared.

The warriors were clad in leather armor and had swords at their hips. She counted five who approached, and another five a little further back.

"What is your business in these mountains?" the leader asked.

"We seek refuge," Zaviana said.

"Seek elsewhere. These mountains are dangerous in the winter."

"We seek the resistance," Zaviana stated.

The man paused as he studied the group accompanying Zaviana. "And what makes you seek them here?"

"I know you are here. And you have a problem ... so does the emperor."

His eyes widened before he straightened himself, giving her a stern look. "What do you know?"

"I will speak with your leader. Danger is coming."

He scanned the villagers one more time. "Very well, follow us."

Warriors approached all around them, walking along their sides and behind as they followed the captain deeper into the mountains.

Zaviana took a deep breath, relieved to have reached the resistance at last. Her only growing concern was how soon the emperor would attack. She supposed it depended on how threatened he was about the resistance. If he truly feared them, he would gather as much of his army as he could before he attacked. That gave them time; however, it also meant if they weren't fast enough, there would be no hope. The empire would crush them.

They followed the warriors through swirls of trails through the mountains until they approached a large gate. Zaviana's eyes widened as she saw the exterior of the city. It was fortified with stone and metal, most likely from the mountain itself. Even if the empire attacked, the city didn't look like it would fall easily.

The gate opened and everyone went inside. Once the last warrior at their rear entered the gate, he signaled, and it closed.

"Welcome to Saefron," the captain said.

"It's incredible," Naveen said.

Zaviana smiled as she looked around. The streets were clear, and several of the buildings appeared deserted. Most were made of stone, but many others were built with wood. She marveled at their appearance. But as she looked around, an unsettling feeling came over her. The city was massive, as large as Melonia, but the streets were empty. It wasn't night, but midday. More people should be in the streets.

"It looks empty ... deserted," she whispered.

The captain glanced at her. "Come. We'll need to see Ellisar in the conference room." He wrinkled his nose at the villagers. "The others will need to stay behind. We don't have room for everyone. They will be taken care of."

"I understand," Zaviana said. "However, I request Naveen accompany us. She speaks for most of the villagers."

"Very well."

Zaviana followed the captain to the center of the city. She took in the sight of the city as she followed, marveling at its beauty, but concern still flooded her with how empty the streets were. Only a handful of women and children littered the streets. She did not like the shivers that traveled down her spine. Something was wrong.

The captain led them inside a large room with a long rectangular table. At the head of the table sat an old man, whose white mustache curled toward his nose. He smiled at them as they sat down.

"Welcome to Saefron. My name is Ellisar. I am the leader of the resistance. I was sent word that you have dire news for me to hear."

Zaviana glanced from Ellisar to the captain. "I'm assuming your captain sent word ahead as we were being escorted here?"

Ellisar nodded.

"And what is your name?" She asked the captain.

"Balderyck. I'm the standing captain while Tynaer is away."

She nodded to him. "First, I want to recognize Naveen here. Her courage is what brought so many villagers to your doorstep today. When her village was attacked by dragonriders, and her friends and companions hung for traitors, she rallied several of the villagers to join her and find you."

Ellisar's bushy white eyebrows rose on his forehead. "The Dragonia Empire is still resorting to murdering villagers?"

Naveen nodded. "Yes, milord. They claim the villagers were resistance sympathizers and traitors to the empire. I knew many of them. They were no such thing. We lived simple lives and did everything we could to remain unnoticed from the empire's eye."

"What village are you from?"

"Anius."

"I had a few followers there, but they were to remain low-key. Do you remember the names of the people they killed?"

She nodded.

"If you could, I would like their names later. I would like to know if I knew any of them."

"As you wish."

"Ellisar, they did this to at least two more villages," Zaviana said.

His eyes widened.

"Dragonriders have been traveling from village to village, accusing people of being traitors, hanging several people from each village, and burning their homes," Zaviana said.

"That is ill news. I don't know what you want from me though. We do not have the power to protect the villages."

"I believe they are instilling fear into the villagers, fear to join you."

"Fear?"

Zaviana nodded. "Yes. And I've asked myself many times ... why would they bother instilling fear in their people?"

He scratched his shaved chin. "And your conclusion?"

"They're scared. People weren't leaving the villages in waves to join you. Many villages thought the resistance was only a rumor. You haven't exactly been recruiting. Until recently, no one has known where you are—"

"Until recently," he interrupted.

"I heard you recently won a battle against the empire. Is that true?"

He nodded. "A battle ... yes. It was unintentional, and it left many casualties. But we did survive it."

"No one ever has, and now the emperor is scared."

"What did you mean when you said until recently no one has known where we are?"

Zaviana inhaled, looked down, then blew out a slow breath. She met Ellisar's eyes. "The emperor knows you're here. You're in danger. In fact, we all are now that we're here."

His eyes nearly bulged out of their sockets. "How? Did you lead them here?"

She shook her head. "I was a prisoner of the emperor ... for many years. I was first captured by two dragonriders collecting taxes from northern farms. My family was killed except for my brother. He was left to spread the news. I was taken. I was intended for the dragonrider, but a mercenary found me. He was on a quest for the empire, tracking down some traitor who stole a stone from the emperor—"

"The dragon stone?"

Zaviana flinched. "Yeah ... the dragon stone. How did you know?"

Ellisar exhaled. "He was supposed to deliver that to me. It would have turned the tide of the war years ago."

Zaviana's lips pressed firmly together. "Well, the mercenary found me and saved me. He killed the dragonrider who tried to force himself on me. The other fled."

"And the dragon?"

"Excuse me?" she asked.

"I've always wondered what happened to the dragon after its rider was killed."

"The dragon shrieked in rage at first, but it left with the other rider when it couldn't defeat Derkas."

"Derkas ... yes, I've heard the name. He has quite the reputation. So what happened to you?"

"We traveled together for a time. He offered his protection, and I was scared, so I clung to him. My emotions were high, and after months of traveling with him in search of this traitor and the stone, I fell for him."

Ellisar didn't show emotion. He simply nodded.

Zaviana gulped. "When we finally found the stone and the man who had stolen it, we brought them back to the emperor. Derkas kept me out of sight, but the emperor sensed me. He came after me. An army of dragonriders surrounded me, and I couldn't fight them. When Derkas was giving the traitor and the stone to the emperor, they captured me and brought me in."

"Why did the emperor seek you out?" Ellisar's index finger rubbed his mustache.

"I don—"

Ellisar jerked upright. "Did you touch the stone?"

"I—" Zaviana broke off. Shivers traveled over her body. A cold sweat overcame her.

"Did you touch the stone?"

She gulped. "Yes."

"Is it true then?"

"Is what true?"

"Did the dragon stone do something to you? Did some of its power transfer over to you?"

Zaviana's lips crunched together. She hadn't realized the leader of the resistance would know so much. Most of the events with Derkas and the dragon stone she had kept secret. No one knew. It was time for her to reveal her longest kept secret.

"Yes."

"Magic ..." Ellisar whispered.

Zaviana nodded.

Ellisar's face remained stoic for a long while, then it split into a grin. "Perhaps the tides are turning after all."

Zaviana shook her head. "I was a prisoner for many years. The emperor studied me, tested me, did many cruel things to me ... all to discover the limits of my abilities. I resisted most of it."

"How did you escape?"

"I didn't. Derkas came back. He traded for me."

"Traded? What could the empire possibly want enough to let you go …" His eyes bulged.

"You. Derkas discovered your location. He told the emperor where you are … and now the Dragonia Empire is coming. They are coming here."

Chapter 13

The conference room filled with silence. No one spoke for several long minutes. The only sound was their heartbeats and breaths, which were mind-numbingly loud. Not one of their hearts beat with the serenity of calm. Each person in the room had a rapid heartbeat, one of worry and fright.

"Coming here?" Ellisar asked at last.

"Yes," Zaviana said. "We need to ready your defenses. You've defeated them once, we need to do so again."

"Defeated them? We've never taken the wrath of the entire Dragonia Empire. If they indeed have discovered where we are, they won't have a mere ten dragonriders. They'll have hundreds. We can't defeat them." Ellisar stood. "We barely defeated the ten dragonriders the last time!"

"But you did defeat them," Zaviana retorted.

"We defeated them with our army ... I don't know if you have noticed, but we are rather without one at the moment."

Zaviana's brows furrowed. "I noticed the streets are empty. I hoped there were more of you. Where is your army?"

Ellisar rubbed his face with both hands. "They're off the west coast of Kaeldroga, on a small island in the south."

Zaviana's mouth dropped open. "What in the blazes are they doing there?"

"Training," Ellisar muttered.

"Why are they training all the way over there? We're on the eastern side of Kaeldroga ... that's months away."

Ellisar nodded. "Yes."

"We're doomed, aren't we? We're all going to die here."

"Perhaps ... perhaps not. We can make the journey by ship in a week if we're lucky."

"A week?" Zaviana asked. "Even if that's true, we'd have to bring them all back, and depending on how many, that'd take at least several weeks, if you even have enough ships for all of them."

"They don't need ships to return."

"Don't need ships?"

"They have wyverns."

Zaviana bit her bottom lip. "Wyverns? What are wyverns?"

"They're flying reptiles similar to dragons ... but a lot smaller."

Zaviana raised an eyebrow. "How much smaller?"

"Instead of an ant riding a lizard, think of an ant riding a grasshopper."

Her brow furrowed. "And you've been training them to ride?"

Ellisar nodded.

"And can they breathe fire like dragons?"

His eyes glowed as a smile found its way onto his face. "Much more. So far, we've discovered wyverns that can breathe fire, ice, acid, lightning, and a powerful wind current."

Zaviana's eyes nearly bulged out of their sockets. "How many?"

Ellisar smiled. "Hundreds."

"Where are they?"

His face fell. "As I said ... they're on a small island many miles off the western bank of Kaeldroga in the south."

Her hand touched her face as she considered his words. "That's why your warriors are so far away. This island must be the wyverns' native land."

"That is correct."

"If they reach us in time, do we stand a chance?" Naveen asked.

"That is hard to say. We've only had one battle so far, and it was twenty wyverns versus ten dragonriders." Ellisar gulped. "And we lost over half."

"It's our only chance," Zaviana said.

"Yes it is. For our sake, I hope they reach us in time ... and I hope we have enough."

"When do we leave?"

He tilted his head. "Leave?"

"You said a ship has to be taken to this island to request the army returns. When do we leave?"

"I'll send men first thing in the morning. Do not concern yourself with it."

"It is my concern. I will accompany them. I will help bring word to your warriors."

"Why? There is no need for you to go. You can help us here."

"I have seen what the Dragonia Empire is capable of. I have seen the dragonriders, the dragons ... and I know what they can do. I need to see these wyverns, their abilities, so I can judge the most effective way to use them."

Ellisar sighed. "Very well. But for now, get some rest." Zaviana and Naveen walked out of the council room, their heads held high. An overwhelming gloom settled upon them as they thought about the Draconia Empire's arrival. But they focused on hope. The red sun set in the west, casting a beautiful scarlet glow over the horizon.

"Would you like to watch the sunset?" Naveen asked.

"It's been a long time since I've seen a sunset," Zaviana said.

"Perhaps we can talk a little bit as well..."

"Yes, we should."

The two of them walked together in silence. Each had burdens weighing on her shoulders as she thought about the implications of the Draconia Empire and the resistance. Neither knew what they were going to do if the resistance were to fail.

"How long were you a prisoner of the emperor?" Naveen asked.

Zaviana took a deep breath, stretched, opened her mouth, and paused to study the sunset for several long moments. "Well, you want to dive right into, don't you?"

"Well, I don't know much about you. I want to know more." Naveen brushed her hand through her long black hair. "I feel a connection with you. I don't know how to explain it, but I have this sense we're meant to be close."

"A sense, you say?" Zaviana asked.

"Yes, I've had an extra sense all my life. My mother called it a gift. My father called it a curse. She had the gift too, you know? But Father was right. When I was a little girl, she let me watch her use her extra sense. The villagers saw and called her witch."

"I'm sorry," Zaviana said.

"When you touched the stone, what did it feel like?"

"It feels like ... pain. An intense amount of pain surged through me. I felt the hottest fire, the coldest ice, the most electric light. It was very painful."

"Is it still painful?"

"Sometimes."

"Before you touched the stone, did you have any abilities at all?" Naveen asked.

Zaviana smiled. "Like you, I had an extra sense."

Naveen's eyes widened. "You did?"

"Yes. There are very few of us to have this extra sense, and in our world, it's a very dangerous sense to have... Especially if someone else finds out. I did learn more about it while a prisoner of the emperor."

"What did you learn?"

"We are rare. I've been able to piece together a lot of things, but you must realize that they never told me anything. I had to put the pieces together myself. I overheard small conversations here and there. I was alone for so long. All I could do was gather as much information as I could."

"I'm sorry you had to endure that. It sounds miserable."

"It was. As far as I could gather, dragons used to be intelligent beings. A long time ago they could communicate with the dragonriders. I've seen them ... the dragons. I don't see any intelligence in them anymore. It's like they are mindless beasts."

"What happened?"

"The dragon stone. The stone from space. I don't know exactly what happened, but the empire, or the emperor, saw the stone drain the life from a dragon. He was intrigued and sent men to touch the stone. They died. Their life force seeped into the stone. Somehow he found a way to touch it. But also he used it to drain the magic and intelligence from all of the dragons. Now, this is just legend, whispers I heard from the guards. I don't know how much of this is true, but if it can be believed, the dragon stone sucks the magic, the power, and intelligence from each dragon after it's born, and it harnesses the energy inside of the stone. The dragons become slaves to the empire. With one touch, the magic from those dragons seeps into the human who touches it. I touched it by accident, and now I can do things. I can feel the moisture in the air. I feel the different temperatures all around me, and I can change the temperatures all around. Fire is easy to make, all you have to do is get something hot enough. Ice, ice is even easier. Do you know how much water there is? I can sense it, I can feel it, I can control it. I can suck moisture out of the air. I can bring it into my embrace and release it like a waterfall. I can feel all the air around me. I can sense it. It's like it's a living creature that wants to be controlled."

"That's incredible. I wish I could touch the stone."

"No, no you don't. Yes, it comes with power, but there is a price. Every time I use it, this magic, I feel weaker. Depending on how much I use, sometimes I can't walk for days. The pain is inconceivable. Every time I use magic, I feel pain. Not hit-your-finger pain, but like I am being stabbed through the guts and the blade twisted. And worst of all, like the stories that I really believe are true, I can see memories, dreams. I have dreams every night I have to use magic. Dreams of flying insects talking to dragons. For you see, in this dream I am a dragon. I'm talking to other dragons. When I wake up every morning, I have the knowledge that my voice and my intelligence has been stripped away. In the dreams I can talk to my friends; I can talk to the other dragons. But once I wake up, the intelligence is gone, ripped away by a single man, all for power. It takes me several minutes to realize it was only a dream, and that I'm not really a dragon. I wonder how much of my dream is reality for the dragons ..."

Naveen reached over and grabbed Zaviana's hand. "You're not alone anymore. I may not have the same power as you, but I'll always be here when you need someone to talk to. We are in this together."

Zaviana squeezed Naveen's hand. "Thank you. There is one more thing I learned while in Melonia."

"What's that?"

"There is power in dragonscales. Not a lot ... but a little. It doesn't work for most people." She reached around her neck and removed a necklace. It sparkled crimson in the sunset. Zaviana handed it to Naveen. "But for those with the extra sense ... it is strong."

Naveen looked at the necklace in her hand. She studied the dragonscale. It was half the size of her hand, and framed in thin silver. "It's beautiful."

"Keep it," Zaviana said.

Naveen shook her head.

"You may need it more than me. I'm leaving tomorrow. You need to stay here and help protect everyone."

Naveen handed it back to her. "I don't need it."

Zaviana's brow furrowed. "We should get some sleep."

Naveen nodded. She reached to her own necklace and gently rubbed it between her fingers. She smiled. "Yes, we should."

Chapter 14

Zaviana glanced behind her one last time at the hidden city of Saefron. She'd said goodbye to Naveen first thing in the morning before daybreak. Zaviana couldn't understand it, but she felt a connection with the woman. She wondered if it had to do with her extra sense, or something else. Zaviana was afraid to leave Saefron, afraid it wouldn't be there when she came back. Yet, somehow, she felt with Naveen staying behind, it was under good hands.

She traveled with a force of twenty, twelve men and eight women. Zaviana was glad to see women in the resistance army. When she was a prisoner in the Dragonia Empire, all she saw were men warriors. Women were nothing but wives and slaves. Perhaps if the resistance won, women would have a proper place in society.

Zaviana lingered for a moment, then had to catch up with the rest of the resistance. They weren't stopping to wait for her as they pushed forward to reach the bay. Time was limited. The Dragonia Empire was coming. She ran to the woman in front, the one who'd organized the trip.

"Lilianya, how far is it to the ship?"

"We will reach it at sunset."

"Sunset?" Zaviana's voice fell.

"We're in the mountains, not a port city."

"I know ... I'm just anxious. And worried."

"All will be well."

"How do you know?" Zaviana asked.

"Because I believe. I have faith."

Zaviana frowned. She kept pace with Lilianya, but neither talked much of the day.

True to her word, the sun's red glow glimmered over the western horizon when they reached the bay in the south. The tension inside of Zaviana relaxed as she saw the ship in the distance. She wanted to sprint down the mountain to the ship, but she stayed back with the rest of the party. Though she fidgeted the whole time. They'd barely made it to the mountain when she felt a shiver along her spine.

Zaviana reached her arm out, blocking Lilianya from stepping forward.

"What are yo—"

"Something is wrong," Zaviana said.

"Ho—"

"*Shh.*"

Zaviana closed her eyes. Chill bumps crawled up her bare arms. Blackness surrounded her. She saw twelve glowing red humanoid shapes inside her mind, six approaching from each side. Her eyes opened, and she unsheathed her sword.

"Danger approaches. Twelve warriors."

Lilianya's brows furrowed, but she didn't speak. Instead, she grabbed a bow and nocked an arrow.

Zaviana clenched her hilt tight as she angled to her left to face her first opponent. Before she reached the warrior, an arrow pierced his chest. He staggered, leaving an opening for Zaviana. She jumped on the opportunity, flicking her sword to the left, knocking the weapon out of the man's grasp. She raised her foot in the air, slamming it into the man's neck. He crumpled to the ground, unconsciousness overtaking him.

Zaviana rushed to the next warrior. She shifted her weapon from side to side, each swing catching the warrior's blade. His attack was fierce. She couldn't work her way around it. Her foot slid on the slick snow. The warrior took advantage, pressing forward with a flurry of strikes. Zaviana couldn't hold her ground. She slipped. Her body slammed into the ground, and her sword clattered by her side. She reached for it, but the warrior stepped on her wrist. His grin showed through his t-visor.

The warrior's sword slashed down toward Zaviana's face. She rolled on top of his foot, dodging the strike. Zaviana slammed her fist into the warrior's groin. He collapsed onto the ground. She rolled away, grabbed her sword, and stood, ready to strike. Another warrior came at her, slamming his sword against hers. The vibrations hurt her wrist, and she dropped her weapon. She staggered backward as he approached her. Zaviana felt the energy all around her, in the air, in the clouds, in the sunset. She clenched her fists and funneled all the energy into her. Fire blazed from her fingertips. The warrior screamed, dropping his sword and falling to the ground.

Zaviana refocused her mind. She transformed the air at her fingertips, sucking all the heat into her body, making all the air at her fingertips freezing cold. She released the cool air. The moisture in the air collected with it, transforming into ice as it collided into the three warriors who surrounded her. Their movements slowed. Zaviana ducked, grabbed the fallen sword lying in front of her, and thrust it upward into the chest of a warrior. His sword was inches from her face, where it froze before dropping from his hands. He collapsed onto the ground.

Zaviana spun around, ready to face whoever was left. There was no one. Arrows protruded from many of the warriors, but several others were cut down by a few of the resistance warriors. Everyone remaining stared at Zaviana with wide eyes and mouths agape.

She dropped the sword and turned away. Zaviana had been able to use magic for a while, but she never did so with so many witnesses around her. She couldn't hide who she was anymore. A hand touched her shoulder. She spun around, clenching the wrist of the woman behind her.

"Zaviana." Lilianya cringed.

Zaviana let go. "I'm sorry. I'm so sorry."

Lilianya rubbed her wrist. "Thank you."

Zaviana raised an eyebrow.

"You saved us."

"You're not scared of me?"

Lilianya smiled. "Why should we be scared? You're on our side."

Zaviana breathed out, relief overcoming her. She'd been so afraid.

"Come on, we'd better hurry to the ship. If there are warriors already here guarding the bay, the rest of the empire's forces can't be too far away."

Zaviana shivered.

Chapter 15

Naveen observed the beautiful sunrise glistening over the mountaintops. She loved the mountains. Before she'd only seen them at a distance from her small village. But now she was atop them. It was more beautiful than she'd ever imagined. She stood in a field, surrounded by flowers and butterflies fluttering all around her. It was peaceful. This was somewhere she could train.

Naveen wished she could have gotten to know Zaviana before she had to leave. She trusted Zaviana, she didn't know how or why, but she trusted her. However, Zaviana was gone, and Naveen felt very alone.

Fraeyn stood before her, a wide grin spread across his face, eyebrows stretched as far as they could go toward his hairline. He was ready. Naveen had seen a little bit of what Fraeyn could do. She knew he had the extra sense, the ability she had. It was hard to explain. She knew things, things that she should not know. Things that no one else knew. She comprehended things. She could sense things before they occured. She knew which way danger was, and what to do when it approached. Fraeyn was similar—he had an extra sense, an extra ability. Together, they would train, they would learn how to access these abilities.

She reached her hand up and touched her necklace. It was hidden beneath her leather armor. But she felt power. Her mother had given her the necklace many years ago. A gift. A gift with a caution. Naveen always wondered if it were the necklace or her that held the extra sense. Her mother had it. But her mother had cautioned her against using it, against letting other people know what she could do. She still remembered the day when her mother and father were hung. Faded memories became flesh and life, terror as she remembered the horrible events of that day.

"Are we ready?" Fraeyn asked.

Naveen nodded. "Yes."

Naveen focused. She closed her eyes and stretched out with her senses. Like her sight, her extra sense, her telepathy sense as she came to regard it, could feel things, it knew things that surrounded her area. It felt like everything in the air was connected, particles in the air all around her. Better than her eyesight, it could detect every particle of dust around her. She stretched her arm in front of her body and commanded the particles to move.

"Arrg."

Naveen opened her eyes. Fraeyn sat on his bottom in the grass in front of her. He looked up at her, his head tilted, his facial expression twisted. "What did you do?"

"I redirected the energy around me."

"You pushed me down with wind. How did you do that? How did you control the wind?"

"I did what?" Naveen asked.

"I watched you. You held your hand in front of you, and a swirl of purple dust, or wind, circled around your hand. Then it sprang forth and shoved into my chest. Now I'm sitting on the ground."

"Incredible."

"How did you do it?" Fraeyn asked.

"I closed my eyes, and I directed my senses. It's like I could feel a bunch of particles all around me. I can't see them with my naked eye, but I can feel them. Thousands of them, all around me. I concentrated on them and redirected them to my hand. Then I released all the particles I collected."

"I don't know if I can do that," Fraeyn said.

"Try."

Fraeyn closed his eyes. He held both of his hands stretched in front of him. One hand wrapped around his opposite wrist. His hand shook, trembled, but his focus was tight. Naveen saw the air all around him move, shift. She watched in utter fascination as it all collected in front of his hand. However, instead of looking like wind, it glowed an orange-red. Naveen opened her mouth to say something, but it was too late. Flames covered his hands. He released the energy. Flames rushed at her. Naveen tried to dodge, but they were too fast. The flames collided with her face and she crumpled to the ground, rolling to try and put herself out.

"Oh no, are you all right? What happened?" he asked.

Naveen brushed off her cloak as she stood. Her eyes were wide, her mind spinning. She looked down at her half-burnt clothes. Thankfully, she wasn't burned.

"You didn't create wind ... you created fire."

"I ... what?" he asked.

He clutched at the neck of his tunic with wide eyes.

"What do you have under your tunic?"

"I made fire?"

"Fraeyn ... answer me."

"What?" he asked.

"What are you clutching?"

He looked down at his hand. His hand released the cloth as he stumbled forward.

"Oh, it's nothing. Are you all right?"

"Do you have a dragonscale necklace?" she asked.

His eyes bulged. "How do you know?"

Naveen reached under her cloak and brought out the necklace her mother gave her. It shimmered a deep purple in the sunlight. The scale was small, no larger than a copper dragon coin. Every time she touched it, she felt like it gave her power, but she'd never believed it was true.

Fraeyn started at her necklace with his mouth open. He reached under his tunic and grabbed a necklace. It glinted red in the sunlight.

Naveen stepped closer to him and each of them gently picked up the other's necklace to inspect.

"Do you think these are real dragonscales?" Fraeyn asked.

"My mother told me mine was, and to keep it secret and safe."

"Mine did as well ... but I didn't believe her. How would my mother have a dragonscale?"

"I believe they were mined in the mountains. At least, that's what my father told me. He said a bunch of miners found a bunch of them inside the mountains when they were collecting minerals. Some of them were used to craft things, but a few of the miners kept some for trinkets. He gave this one to my mother."

"Do you think the dragonscale has something to do with our abilities?" he asked.

"I'm not sure ..."

"Our scales are different colors. I've seen red dragons before ... but never a purple one."

Naveen smiled. "Father told me it was the only purple one they found in the mines, and that he was the one who found it."

"Do you think the color of the scales has something to do with the magic?" Fraeyn asked.

Naveen raised an eyebrow. "What do you mean?"

"Well, we've both seen red dragons. They breathe fire. My scale is red, and I created fire."

Naveen's jaw dropped. "I created wind. Do you think if there are purple dragons out there that they can't breathe fire?" Naveen paused. "Didn't you tell me when you saw me create wind that it glowed purple?"

He nodded. "It did."

"Incredible."

Fraeyn grinned. "We need to practice more."

"Agreed."

Chapter 16

Zaviana sat alone in her cabin, a quilt wrapped around her shoulders. She'd ridden on the back of a dragon, traveled by horseback, and been inside a wagon, but none of those had prepared her for being on a ship. The constant side to side motion of the waves pounding against the hull of the ship made her stomach turn. She tried to fight it, but more often than not, she found herself huddled over a bucket in the corner. After the third day, it got better, but she still didn't like traveling by ship. She wondered how much time they had. Surely the empire would strike soon. Would they make it in time? Could they save the resistance? Zaviana wasn't so sure.

Everyone worked hard on the oars and manned the sails, but even with their best efforts, they were still another two days from where the rest of the resistance hid. Zaviana didn't like it. Why would they split apart so far?

She closed her eyes to concentrate. They would make it; they had to. If it took five days to reach the rest of the resistance, and another five to return, with a possible one or two-day delay in the middle ... more than ten days. She didn't know how they would make it. The empire wouldn't wait ten days to attack would they?

Zaviana rocked back and forth, itching for something to do, some way to contribute. There had to be something. But she was stranded, stuck on a ship, one in constant motion, rocking back and forth, back and forth. She shook her head, trying to clear her thoughts. There had to be something, anything she could focus on.

Her magic.

She could focus on her magic. Zaviana closed her eyes and concentrated. The particles all around her glimmered in her head. She saw a three-dimensional representation of them all around her. There was more detail inside her head than with her own eyes. It was incredible. She'd never had so much time to concentrate, to focus on her power and the power floating all around her. Energy. Everything that surrounded her was energy. Moisture, heat, sand, dust, static, and so much more. They surrounded her. Each element radiated a different color light inside of her head. Red for heat, blue for moisture, silver for cold, tan for earth. The wood around her in the cabin was full of energy as well. She'd believed the ship to be dead, the remnants of long-ago trees, but as she reached out and separated the particles, she realized the wood absorbed energy. Heat, moisture, and anything else that could squeeze through the pores of the wood was there.

Zaviana grinned. With her mind, she could separate the particles, focusing on individual particles and pushing them to her will. She held her hand in front of her. Her eyes remained closed, but she focused on her hand. There was no darkness in her mind; it was full of colors, millions of them. She moved the particles of wind away from her hand and funneled moisture and cold, compacting it into a solid ball. Her teeth gritted, but she didn't waver. She continued compressing the energy, until, at last, she felt the cold in her palm. Startled, she opened her eyes. Inside of her hand was a ball of solid ice the size of her palm. Her eyes widened. She'd created ice. Zaviana had intentionally created ice.

A knock on the door startled her. She flinched, and the ball of ice dropped to the floor, shattering on impact.

"Zaviana?" a voice asked.

"Come in," Zaviana said.

Lilianya stepped inside, closing the door behind her. Her eyebrows furrowed as she glanced at the ground. "What?"

"Can I help you?" Zaviana asked.

"Is that ice on the ground?"

"Yes."

"How'd you get ice inside of here to last?"

"It is winter," Zaviana responded. "It's probably snowing."

"It is ... outside."

Zaviana shrugged.

"Did you ... make ice?"

"I might have ..."

Lilianya shook her head.

"Is there something I can do for you?" Zaviana asked.

"I was going to let you know we should reach the island tomorrow."

Zaviana's eyes lit up. "Tomorrow?"

"Yes. We're a day ahead of schedule."

"Good."

"I was wondering ..." Lilianya trailed off.

"What is is?" Zaviana asked.

"Could you teach me what you do? Um ... magic?"

Zaviana laughed. "Magic isn't something you can teach. At least, not that I know of. When I was young, I felt something, an extra sense that no one else had. My parents told me to keep it a secret. They told me people wouldn't understand. Therefore, for the longest time, I didn't practice it."

"An extra sense? How so?" Lilianya asked.

"I knew when bad things were going to happen before they did. I knew when good things were coming. I knew which way to go to avoid danger."

"How did you know? What did it feel like? A tingle, a shiver? A feeling deep inside your gut that if you chose one path, it would shatter your hopes and dreams? So you decided against it, and traveled a different path?"

Zaviana tilted her head. "Yes."

"Teach me," Lilianya pleaded.

"I—I don't know how. And—"

"What?" Lilianya asked.

"It was only a sense, there was no power that came with it ... That came later."

"When? When did it come?" Lilianya asked.

"When I touched the dragon stone," Zaviana said.

Lilianya raised an eyebrow. "Dragon stone?"

"Yes," Zaviana admitted.

"Where is this dragon stone?"

"The emperor has it."

Lilianya's eyes bulged. "So ... what you're saying is the emperor may have an army of people like you? An army of magicians?"

Zaviana shivered. "I do not know ... perhaps."

"How do we stand a chance?" Lilianya asked.

"There is always a chance. Don't give up hope."

"Hope ... hope seems to be all we have," Lilianya muttered.

Zaviana closed her eyes, focused her energy on all the red particles surrounding her, channeled them all onto her palm, and opened her eyes. A small ball of flame appeared in her hand. "Perhaps hope is all we need."

Chapter 17

Naveen strode into the cordwainer's shop. Cederic stood at the counter, twirling a pair of lasting pliers in his hand. He jerked backward, dropping the tool on the counter. Naveen smiled at him.

Saefron already had a shoemaker, but the man was old, and Cederic had begun working for him. It didn't seem like it would be long before he would make all the shoes. However, at the moment, he seemed to be bored.

"No business?" Naveen asked.

"Well, I sewed a few shoes earlier this morning. But they were just repairs. It seems most of the work is metal boots, which is a little outside of my expertise."

Naveen's bottom lip puffed outward. "Don't you want to learn how to make them though?"

"Well, yeah ... but Onaeron won't let me yet. He says he wants to teach me a few techniques with leather first before I learn something new. He says it's because he doesn't want to confuse me since there are distinct differences between leather shoes and metal boots."

Naveen meandered over to the counter. "Well, I don't know if I would like metal shoes. They seem too clunky for me. Perhaps you could help me then." She raised her eyebrows.

His eyes glowed and a smile came across his face. "Do you need new shoes?"

"I do. My current ones aren't comfortable, and they're beginning to fall apart."

"How aren't they comfortable?" he asked.

"They're stiff. When I walk in them too long, my feet hurt."

Cederic's face brightened. "Well, that could be several different things. Perhaps whoever made your shoes didn't work the leather, or they could have not padded it. Come to the back room and we'll have a look."

Naveen followed Cederic behind the counter and to the back room. Shoes lined the walls along the floor and on shelves.

"Sit," Cederic said.

Naveen raised an eyebrow, then complied, finding a small bench against the wall of the room. As soon as she was seated, Cederic got down on one knee and grabbed her leg. At first, Naveen was startled. She nearly kicked him.

He smiled. "Easy."

Cederic removed her left shoe. He inspected it carefully, running his hands along the leather and feeling it inside and out. His lips pressed together tight and he nodded.

"The craftsmanship of this shoe is lacking. Whoever made it didn't stretch out the leather, nor beat it to loosen its stiffness."

"You're supposed to beat leather?"

"Only the sole. It makes it softer, a little more cushion against your foot. However, with how stiff this is, it's obvious no such thing was done."

Naveen nodded.

"What type of shoe would you like to replace these with?"

"Whatever you have is fine."

"We keep a few common sizes in stock, but no, I'll make you new shoes. We want to make sure they're comfortable, and your feet are a bit smaller than the common man's."

"Well, what do you suggest?"

"What are you planning on doing with them?"

"What do you mean?" Naveen asked.

"Well, I don't imagine you'd be a seamstress or cook. I don't know you too well, but I'd wager you want to go out and do something."

Naveen smiled. "A simple life isn't for me. It never has been."

Cederic waited patiently.

"I want to practice with a sword. Maybe even a bow."

He nodded. "Something a little more sturdy than cowhide then. We need a material that will last longer and be comfortable for your feet."

Naveen tilted her head.

Cederic raised her foot up to look at it closely. He ran his hands along the top and bottom of her foot. She shivered. It didn't tickle ... it felt nice. He pulled out a measuring stick from his pouch and used it on her foot. Cederic measured the width, length, and thickness of each foot. All the while Naveen shivered, warmth spreading through her.

"All right. I believe I have all the measurements I need. I'll have you a new pair of shoes in two days."

"Is that it?"

Cederic nodded, his eyes fixating on a spot on the ground. A touch of sadness touched his eyes. Naveen didn't want to go, at least, not without him. She enjoyed his company.

"Can you use a sword?" she asked.

"A sword?" he asked.

She nodded.

"I've never tried."

"Would you like to?" she asked.

He raised an eyebrow. "When?"

"Now." She smiled.

Naveen held the door open for him. His face lit up as he beamed at her, meeting her gaze.

"I'd love to."

NAVEEN SWUNG HER SWORD forward in a downward arc. Cederic caught it with his own weapon, then slid it down and stepped backward. Naveen had to reposition herself to block his incoming strike. Sweat trickled down her forehead. She'd watched many sparring matches, and she thought she had a general concept of how to wield a sword, but it was harder than she'd imagined. Naveen didn't know if she and Cederic were doing it right, but nonetheless, it was a taxing workout.

They circled each other, silent as they could be, practicing in the meadow outside of Saefron. They didn't want an audience, especially with how bad they each imagined themselves being with a sword.

Cederic rushed at her, three swift slashes with his weapon: right, left, right. Naveen caught the first two, but the third—she slipped. His blade angled down to her hilt and spun the weapon out of her grasp. It tumbled to the ground, as did she after it. Cederic brought his sword down toward her, but she rolled to the side, slamming her feet into his legs. He crumpled to the ground, dropping his weapon. She reached over, grabbed her short sword, climbed on top of him, and held the weapon in front of his throat. A face-splitting grin came across her face.

"Perhaps I'm decent with a sword after all."

Cederic's eyes were wide. He watched her carefully, inspecting, hungry. Naveen dropped the sword to her side. She tried to get up, but her foot slipped on the grass. Her head collided with his chest. She put one hand on the grass and the other on his hard, muscled chest. What was a Cederic doing with such defined muscles? She looked up to his face. It was inches from hers, and he was breathing heavily. Naveen shivered. She licked her lips, studied the cool frost coming from his breath, and got to her feet. She turned away from him, not trusting herself to look at him just yet.

"I told you I'm no good with a sword." He brushed the dirt off of his.

Naveen turned around, a grin on her face, warmth spreading across her cheeks. "I think you are better than you believe."

He raised an eyebrow. "Is that so?"

She nodded. "Would you like to practice again tomorrow?"

He nodded. "I would."

"I'll meet you here at sunset," Naveen said.

Chapter 18

A knock at the door awoke Zaviana. She slid off her uncomfortable cot to rest her feet on the unsteady ground. The knock persisted. She yawned, staggered toward the door, and opened it.

Lilianya stood there, a wide grin across her face. "We're here."

Zaviana yawned. "We've arrived to the island?"

Lilianya nodded. "We're about to be pushed in."

Zaviana's brow furrowed. "Pushed?"

"Yes. You may want to find a sea—"

The entire room shifted, thrown forward at an incredible speed. Lilianya crashed into Zaviana. They tumbled to the ground, Lilianya landing on top of Zaviana. Lilianya's orange hair fell over Zaviana's face, and she nearly choked on it. She spit it out of her mouth and inhaled a deep breath. Roses and strawberries entered her nostrils. Were the scents from Lilianya's hair? It was a wonderful sensation. Lilianya rolled off of Zaviana so both of the women lay on their backs.

The ship's momentum was too strong for either of them to get up, so instead, they looked at each other, helpless. Zaviana noticed how blue Lilianya's eyes were, like shimmers of lake waters. The woman was quite beautiful, for a pale woman.

The ship's movement abruptly stopped, jerking both of the women. Zaviana groaned.

"Is it over?"

"It should be," Lilianya replied.

"What was that?"

"They arrived before I suspected."

"Who arrived?"

"The wyverns."

"Wyverns?"

Lilianya smiled. "Let's just say some of our wyverns have very strong breath."

Zaviana stood, brushed off her tunic, and helped Lilianya to her feet.

"Are you ready to meet them?"

"The wyverns?"

"Yes ... and the rest of the resistance."

Zaviana smiled. "I'm ready."

Lilianya led Zaviana out of the cabin and to the top of the ship. The ramp had already been lowered off the ship, and several of the men on board began unloading the crates of food. Zaviana followed Lilianya to the edge of the ship, then paused.

Wyverns circled the skies in front of her. Not dozens of them, but hundreds, maybe even thousands. Zaviana's jaw dropped.

Lilianya turned around. She watched Zaviana's expression and smiled. "Incredible, aren't they?"

"How many are there?"

"We don't know. Thousands probably. We have over seven hundred trained wyvernriders right now. But we have no idea how many there are." She turned to watch the sky. "We see hundreds of them in the skies that we haven't met yet."

Zaviana's mouth was wide open. She flinched, then closed her mouth. Her hand pushed through her long hair, pushing it behind her ear.

"Come, you need to meet the rest of the resistance. If things are as dire as you say, we need to let them know."

Zaviana nodded. She followed Lilianya off the ramp and to a line of waiting men. A shiver ran down her spine as her feet touched the solid ground. She paused, closed her eyes, and reached out with her senses. She could see the wyverns in her mind, and they resembled the same colors she'd seen with her eyes. They radiated power. Energy flowed inside of them, much like the energy inside of her, the energy she could sense all around her. They had power. She reached her hand to touch her necklace absentmindedly before she opened her eyes and caught up to Lilianya.

A man approached them.

"Hello, I am Tynaer, captain of the resistance's army. And you are?"

"Zaviana."

"The ship captain here tells me you were sent here to tell us some ill news."

"Yes. The resistance is in danger."

The captain looked around, glancing at the wyverns in the sky and the hundreds who had riders on their backs. He turned back to face her.

"Not here. Saefron is in danger. There is—"

He held up his hand to silence her. "Hold off on your explanation. Let me call an emergency council meeting and you can explain it to all of us."

She nodded.

"You must be hungry after traveling this far. Would you care for anything to eat?"

"Please ... but not fish."

He laughed. "You must be tired of fish after the ship."

Tynaer led Zaviana into the city, most of which was still being built. She watched with interest as men and woman alike helped each other with wood and stone to erect buildings. Men and woman gathered in a small field, where they practiced archery and swordsmanship. Wyvernriders flew in the sky practicing aerial combat, including the wyverns using elemental powers from fire to ice, and even warriors practicing sword fighting in the air. Zaviana had a hard time looking away. There were thousands of people here. This island made Saefron look like a ghost town. Why were there still so many people in Saefron, when this island was clearly the safest place? She decided she would ask that question at the meeting.

They went into a large hexagonal stone building. Inside was full of weapons. Most of them looked new, and there were hundreds of them. Zaviana gaped as she looked at the walls. As far as she knew, the wyverns were a new discovery. How had they amassed so many weapons already?

Tynaer held open a door and Zaviana nodded to him as she stepped inside a large room dominated by a huge wooden table. Lilianya followed behind her. The table was already filled with several people. She found a seat.

A few more minutes went by as people continued to file in to fill eleven of the twelve chairs. They all waited in mostly silence, with some of the councilmen whispering to each other. A few were wondering what the meeting was about, while others were discussing local happenings.

A man stumbled into the room backwards, a plate in his hand and a scroll between his teeth. He wavered as he tried to find his balance. His complexion was dark and there was something very familiar about him, but Zaviana couldn't see his face. He turned around, set the scroll on the table, and held out a plate with a steaming steak on top of it.

"Sorry I'm late. Someone told me to bring steak?"

He paused as he scanned the room. His eyes met Zaviana's. They bulged. A wide grin split his face.

"Zavi?" he asked.

"Devarius," she choked out.

She jumped up from her seat and rushed over to meet him. Her arms wrapped around his neck to embrace him in a hug so hard that he gagged for breath. She reluctantly let go of her death grip.

"Is it really you?" he asked, his eyes watering.

"It is me."

Everyone stared at the two of them for a long moment, until someone in the room cleared their throat.

Devarius shook his head. "Sorry ... everyone, this is my sister."

Several gasps filled the air, and then smiles filled everyone's face.

Devarius made everyone shift seats until he could sit by his sister. The two looked at each other for a long moment.

"All right. Zaviana, would you mind telling us what this is all about? What danger it is that we face?" Tynaer asked.

Zaviana looked away from her brother and nodded. "The empire has learned where the resistance has been hiding."

Devarius' eyes bulged. "They're coming here?"

Zaviana shook her head. "No. They don't know where this is. I don't even know where this is. But they learned about Saefron."

"How?" Tynaer asked.

"It's a bit of a long story. I'll need to fill you in on a little background about me." Zaviana looked around the room. "As all of you now know, I am Devarius' sister. The Dragonia Empire came to our farm when Devarius was young and I was almost a woman. They killed our parents and my older brother. We couldn't afford taxes that year. After a hard freeze, most of our crops had died, and we barely had enough food for ourselves. That didn't matter to the empire. They left Devarius, probably to tell the tale about what happens when you don't pay the empire taxes. But they took me. One of the dragonriders took a liking to me."

Devarius snarled.

Zaviana's eyes lowered. "What he would have done with me ... I do not know. I don't imagine I would have got away easily, or at all. However, someone else found me. He saw the dragonriders and how they treated me, how I was their prisoner. And before they could take advantage of me, he came to my rescue. He killed the dragonrider. The other fled and the remaining dragon went crazy, burning up some of the village before flying away."

"Who saved you?" Devarius asked.

"A man by the name of Derkas."

Devarius tilted his head. "The mercenary?"

Zaviana's cheeks reddened. "Yes. He wasn't well known at the time, but he was on a quest for someone who betrayed the emperor. He was on his way to find the resistance and give them information."

Tynaer nodded. "Yes. He caught the man, and because of him, we had to wait many more years until we could stand a chance to fight back."

Zaviana dipped her head. "I know. I was traveling with him during this journey. I disagreed with him. I told him the empire was corrupt, and they deserved to fall. He agreed, but refused to give up the chance for the money. He said we could run away from it all and live like a queen and king ..."

"He fell for you?" Devarius asked.

Zaviana nodded. "And I for him. When he captured the runaway, he brought him back to the emperor. He had me hide. He was worried the empire would try to take me again. He received his bounty, but when he returned, I was gone. The empire had found me."

The room was silent as they watched her, waiting for the conclusion of her story.

"I was brought before the emperor. They had seen me traveling with the mercenary, and saw what I could do. I was a special prisoner of the emperor's and he studied me. For years I was in Dragonia as a slave."

Devarius wiped a tear from his eye. "Why was the emperor so intrigued by you?"

"Because of my abilities."

"What abilities?" Devarius asked.

Zaviana looked around the room and studied each person. They all watched her closely. She held out her hand, and a small ball of ice formed in her palm. Blue frost sizzled from it as she placed it on the table.

"Magic?" Devarius asked.

"Yes, though it wasn't this advanced when I was his prisoner."

"How did you escape?" Devarius asked.

"One day, I was set free. To my surprise, Derkas was the one awaiting me. He ransomed my freedom. In exchange for my freedom, he told the emperor the location of the resistance. He's the one who found Saefron."

"That no-good—" Tynaer mumbled.

"He's a scoundrel, I know that. But twice he saved me from the empire. If he hadn't told them, I would still be a prisoner."

"Well, if for nothing else, I am thankful to him for that," Devarius said.

"What do we do?" Tynaer asked.

"We gather all the wyverns and all the warriors, and we make haste to reach Saefron," Devarius said.

"What if we're too late?" Tynaer asked.

"We have to try. I for one cannot sit back and let them die," Devarius said.

Tynaer shook his head. "Nor can I. I'm just worried that we're not ready."

"If we keep waiting, we'll never be ready," a young man across from Devarius said.

"Agreed," Devarius said. "At least if we can make it to Saefron before the attack, we'll be able to prepare the defense."

"If we make it before the attack," Tynaer grumbled.

"Have faith, Captain."

Tynaer took a deep inhalation of breath through his nose. He closed his eyes and tilted his head back. "Have it your way, Devarius."

Devarius grinned.

"We'll leave in the morning," Tynaer said.

Chapter 19

Naveen waved her arms around in a circle, distorting the air. Her purple dragonscale necklace dangled loose now, which seemed to amplify her power. Air from all around her funneled toward her hands as she collected it. She could see the air particles as easily with her eyes open as when she closed them now. Once enough was collected, she released her power. A blast of wind crushed into the small metal bucket over a hundred paces away. It sprang into the air, up higher than any building before it spiraled down.

"Neat," Fraeyn said.

Naveen beamed. "That was fun."

"Do it again."

She shook her head. "I want to conserve my strength. This is still new and it uses a lot of energy. Besides, it's your turn."

"Are you sure I can do this?" he asked.

Naveen nodded. "Definitely. All it takes is practice."

"I don't know ..."

"Well, I do. You need to have more faith in yourself."

Fraeyn looked down at his feet.

Naveen sprinted toward the fallen tin can. She set it back on the tree stump and egged him on. He motioned for her to step further out of the way. Naveen knew he was nervous about his power, especially since they'd learned he could channel fire. Her ability, air, seemed a little less dangerous. He touched his necklace, closed his eyes, and brought his hands in front of him. The air around him distorted. She noticed the air around her grow colder, as if he were draining what little heat surrounded them. She wondered if that were true, and if so, if he'd use less energy in the summer.

Fraeyn's hands glowed red, and the air in front of him turned a translucent orange. He opened his eyes, and Naveen could have sworn they appeared red as well. The fireball flew from his hands. His mouth dropped as it smashed into the tin can. A blinding light flashed through the air. Naveen had to close her eyes. When she opened them, the tin can was gone. She glanced up to the sky, but didn't see it there either. Stunned, she tiptoed to where the tree stump had been. Her eyes bulged when she realized not only was the tin can gone, but so was the tree stump. In its place was a hole, with a pile of melted metal at the bottom.

Fraeyn stepped by her side. He gasped when he looked at the hole. "Did I do that?"

"It appears so ..." Naveen whispered.

Smoke filled the air from the hole. The two of them stepped back. They couldn't believe their eyes.

"Unbelieva—"

A noise came from behind them, startling them. Naveen turned around first, then tackled Fraeyn to the ground before he could protest. A sword filled the air where they had both stood. Several men approached them. She rolled, feeling for her scabbard. It wasn't there. She'd left her weapon back in Sae-fron.

Naveen rolled as another sword strike came toward her. She regretted leaving her weapon behind, but she hadn't thought they'd be in danger so close to Saefron. Apparently, she'd been wrong.

Fraeyn rolled out of the way of a sword slamming toward his head. He felt at his belt and unsheathed a dagger. The next sword angling toward him, he blocked with the small dagger. Rolling toward the warrior, he swept his leg into the man's feet. The warrior fell. Fraeyn rolled on top of him, slamming his dagger into the man's chestplate. He let go of his weapon and grabbed the dying warrior's sword by his side.

Naveen got to her knees, then ducked as another sword swung toward her neck. Once it passed, she got to her feet and slammed her hands into the chest of the warrior. Air slammed with her. She hadn't intentionally channeled air, but it came. It wasn't as powerful as normal, but she was thankful it was there. The man flew backward over ten feet. She stood and took in her surroundings.

Four warriors stood, each with swords raised in front of them. One warrior lay on the ground at Fraeyn's feet. There were five empire warriors this close. Were there others? Naveen looked around. She couldn't see anyone else. Perhaps they were a scouting party, but why did they come after her and Fraeyn? Maybe they thought they were easy prey. After all, she wasn't even armed. At least, as far as they knew.

"What are you doing here?" she asked.

One of the warrior's smiled through his t-visor. "We've come to end resistance scum like you."

"Can you not see the corruption of the empire?" she asked.

He snarled. "The empire is not corrupt. You are the ones rebelling against them. You are the traitors. The empire has been nothing but fair."

Naveen scoffed.

The man rushed at her.

Naveen brought all the air she'd been collecting to her hands. They turned purple as the energy left her, slamming into the chest of the man. He flew backward over a hundred feet, skipping against the ground all the while.

The remaining three warriors glanced at each other nervously.

Naveen reached down to grab the weapon the warrior had left behind during his flight. She didn't wait for the men to rush her; she stepped forward, slashing the weapon in the air. Fraeyn followed her lead, attacking the man in front of him.

Her weapon danced in the air, balancing perfectly between the two warriors who fought her. She glanced to see Fraeyn only fighting one. Naveen wondered if two attacked her because they thought she was the weaker of the two. She'd have to prove them wrong.

Naveen's weapon swung from left to right, first blocking one warrior, then the other. She didn't have much time for any elegant moves, not that she knew many, when she battled two warriors. Most of her parries were overhand, and it was tiring her quickly. She kept her left leg in front of the other, knees slightly bent, and shoulders steady. Naveen dared not slip in her stance—to do so could cost her life.

Her attackers increased their speed, and they made effort to sync their attacks to make it impossible for her to block.

Her foot slipped. She closed her eyes and dropped to the ground. Two swords crisscrossed in the air where her head had been. When her bottom hit the ground, she pulled energy from the air around her and directed it to the head of the warrior at her right. It slammed into him, jerking his neck backward. A snap filled the air as he crumpled to the ground. Naveen rolled, held her hand out, and pushed the air near her to push the warrior's sword to her grasp. With two swords in her possession, she brought them each over her shoulder, crossing her arms, then slammed them together at the standing warrior's knees. He yelled out in pain as he crumpled to the ground. She stood, then plunged one of the swords into his chest.

A grunt echoed to her left. She turned to see Fraeyn on the ground. Naveen tensed, gripped her remaining sword tight, and prepared to help. Before she could take two steps, the air grew cold, and flames protruded from Fraeyn's fingertips. The flames covered the remaining warrior, and he shrieked as he was being burned alive.

Naveen tiptoed toward Fraeyn. He looked to her, his eyes still blazing red.

"Fraeyn? It's me. Naveen."

His eyes lost their red hue, becoming hazel once more. He closed his eyes, his breath coming in gasps.

"Are you all right?" she asked.

He held out his left arm. A deep gash crossed his forearm, blood oozing out of it. Naveen's eyes widened. She dropped to the ground in front of him. Reaching under her leather armor, she ripped some of her cloth underclothes. She closed her eyes and searched the wound. Using the air, she removed as much dirt as she could from his cut, then she opened her eyes and wrapped the cloth around it. She tied it as tight as she could.

"We need to get you back to Saefron."

He nodded, trembling. Naveen helped him to his feet. She glanced down at the warrior he'd defeated. His armor was still intact, but his flesh was gone, only bones remaining. She cringed and looked away.

She studied the bodies around them. Four warriors lay dead. She'd stabbed two and broken the neck of the third with air, and the fourth had been burned alive by Fraeyn. Her eyes bulged. Four. She glanced around, searching for the fifth warrior. He was nowhere to be found. She remembered tossing him over a hundred feet away with air. He wasn't where she'd left him. She guided Fraeyn to the spot where he'd been and looked to the ground. The grass was pressed down. He'd been there.

"The fifth warrior is gone," she whispered.

"What?" he asked.

"There were five who attacked us. I see only four bodies."

"Where did the other go?" Fraeyn asked.

"I don't know. Come, we've got to get back into Saefron and tell the others the empire is here."

Chapter 20

Zaviana watched as crate after crate was brought onto the ships. Besides the one she had traveled on, there were four more ships. It was enough to load a few thousand warriors on, and a lot of supplies. She noticed the men were extra careful with the small crates.

"What's in those crates?" Zaviana asked her brother.

Devarius looked at the crates being loaded onto the ships and smiled. "Those, my sister, are my latest experiment."

Zaviana wrinkled her nose.

"What?" he asked.

"You were never an alchemist. In fact, if I remember correctly, the few potions you tried to make didn't go so well."

Devarius shrunk into his shoulders. "I told Ma I was sorry."

"Sorry? You burned down the barn. Twice."

He smiled. "I helped rebuild it."

Zaviana shook her head. "All right. I'll bite. What's in the crates? What is your latest, entirely safe, experiment?"

Devarius grinned. "If you haven't noticed, not all of these wyverns are the same. There are a few distinct colors."

"Yes, I noticed that. Purple, red, blue, green, and gold."

"Also black."

Zaviana raised an eyebrow. "Black?"

"We've only seen two black wyverns. And neither has approached us, so we are unsure of their abilities."

"Abilities?"

"Not all wyverns breathe fire, sister."

"I saw a few in the skies, one seemed to breathe ice."

Devarius nodded. "Yes. Each color holds a certain element. I'm not sure why, but I've been able to study them. We have ice wyverns, fire, acid, lightning, and wind."

"Wind?" she asked.

"A wind wyvern is the one who blew you to the island."

"Oh, yes ... I remember that unpleasant experience."

Devarius grinned. "Sorry. Make sure you're seated on the ship journey back. The wind wyverns are going to be blowing the ships forward."

Zaviana's eyes bulged.

"It cuts a three-day trip to one."

"One?" she whispered.

Devarius nodded.

"You're avoiding my question."

"Right. Well, I've learned why each wyvern has a certain element. There is a small hole in the bottom of their uvula that excretes liquid. When that liquid mixes with their breath, either hot, cold, or electric, it creates the element."

"Do I need to ask why you were so close to their uvula? Inside a mouth full of teeth?"

"You need not ask, no."

"I thought not."

"Well, anyway, as it turns out, if you gently massage the uvula, oil drips out of it."

"Massage their uvula? Devarius ... you did not?"

He shrugged. "That's beside the point. What matters is, you can collect their oil."

"And why are you telling me all this?" she asked.

He shrugged. "You asked."

Her eyebrows met her hairline. "Wait. Are you telling me those crates—"

"Are full of vials of wyvern oil."

"What does the oil do?"

"Well, a small drop of the fire oil creates a massive flame. A small drop of ice oil will freeze anything it touches. The acid oil will eat through anything it touches. And the lightning oil is shocking." He raised his eyebrows several times.

Zaviana rolled her eyes at the pun. "What about the wind?"

He crunched his lips together and shifted them from side to side. "They don't have oil. The wind wyverns just have incredible lungs."

"Interesting."

"What I am most curious about is the black wyverns."

"How about you don't try to stick your head inside any strange wyvern's mouth?"

Devarius grinned.

"How many vials are there?"

"Hundreds."

"Hundreds?"

He held his finger three centimeters apart. "They're small. You don't need much to do damage. I didn't want to make large vials. I figured it'd be a waste of oil."

"There are so many possibilities with these as a weapon."

Devarius nodded. "Yes, I've already used them as weapons."

"When?"

"The first time we had to face dragonriders. When I dropped ice oil on a dragon, its entire body was encased in ice. Fire oil caught them aflame. Each oil I used was very effective."

"Perhaps hope isn't as lost as I feared."

"Hope is never lost. Besides, we also have hundreds of wyvernriders. And we've been training."

"Good."

Devarius glanced around. "You best get to your ship, sister. We're about to leave."

Zaviana turned to the ships to notice everything was packed. Wyverns took to the air all around the ship, including dozens of purple wyverns flying close by.

"Aren't you coming?"

"I'll be flying."

"Flying?" she asked.

A small blue wyvern flapped its wings above them as it descended to land next to her brother. It stood as tall as a house, but was still a good bit smaller than most of the others. The wyvern's scales glittered in the sunlight. It was gorgeous.

"Zavi, meet Ayla. She's my wyvern, and I'm her rider."

"Ayla," Zaviana whispered.

She reached up to touch the wyvern's nose. A tingle flowed through her body.

Hello, Devarius' sister, a soft feminine voice said inside of her head.

Zaviana's mouth dropped. "You ... you ..." She cleared her throat. "You can talk?"

The wyvern nodded.

Zaviana closed her mouth.

"Introduce yourself," Devarius said.

Zaviana shivered. "I'm Zaviana. It's a pleasure to meet you, Ayla."

The pleasure is mine, Zaviana.

Chapter 21

Naveen grinned as she looked down at Cederic. She offered a hand, which he accepted gratefully. They'd been practicing with swords for over an hour. He'd been getting better, but she still bested him. Both of them were still far from being a master with a sword. Naveen would have preferred to spar out of the city so no one would see them or, more importantly, their lack of skill, but after the attack, everyone had been forbidden from leaving the city.

Saefron was once a happy city, full of positive energy even with the ill news of the Dragonia Empire arriving, but after the attack, everyone was on edge. It was understandable, but the gloom was making Naveen depressed. She was glad she could focus her energy on practicing swords with Cederic. And she was really loving her new shoes. She wiggled her toes again inside after she helped Cederic up. Her whole life, she'd never known shoes could be so comfortable.

"Thanks." Cederic blushed.

Naveen smiled. "Anytime."

"I believe I'm done for the day. I need to rest. You're improving a lot."

"As are you," Naveen responded.

He shrugged. "I don't believe I'll ever be good with a sword."

She laughed. "I'm no expert either. We'll get there."

He wrinkled his nose. His mouth opened like he was about to respond, but instead his eyes grew wide.

"What is it?" she asked.

He ran toward her, tackling her to the ground. Naveen tried to get up, but he held her down, shielding her from the sky. She fought back, but stopped when a shadow passed overhead, blocking out the glow of the red sun. Shivers traveled along her spine. When the shadow disappeared, light flooded the streets.

Cederic rolled off of her. She glanced to the sky but didn't see anything.

"What was that?" she asked.

"A dragon ..."

She glanced around, eyes wide, until she spotted the beast in the sky, heading back toward them. Naveen grabbed his hand and pulled him away. Fire blazed through the sky, scorching the ground where Cederic had just stood.

His eyes were wide in shock. He quivered.

"Thank you."

She smiled. "I'm just returning the favor."

"We better get out of here. Our mediocre sword fighting isn't going to do anything to a dragon."

Her smile turned upside down. "They're here too soon. Zaviana isn't back yet."

Cederic shook his head. "I don't think they're going to be back in time. They've had to travel too far. We may have to fight alone."

Naveen bit her lip. "We won't win."

He shook his head. "No, we won't."

Naveen looked back up into the sky. Three dragons circled overhead, but only one came close enough to the city to be a threat. As the dragon nosedived, arrows sprung into the air. Naveen turned around to see over a dozen archers with arrows nocked. More arrows released into the air. Most of them bounced off the scales of the dragon, but one penetrated the dragon's wing.

"The wing!" she shouted.

All the archers glanced her way. "Aim for the dragon's wings!"

She didn't need to say it again. All the archers loosed again. Arrows fluttered into the horizon. Several missed, and several more bounced harmlessly off the underbelly scales, but a few more penetrated into the wings of the beast.

Naveen smiled. Her smile faded as the dragon flew closer. She grabbed Cederic's arm, turned around, and ran. Fire plummeted into the ground, burning in a straight line. Men and women screamed. Naveen spun around briefly to see several of the archers' charred remains. The remaining archers ran. Fire burned the ground in a straight line, building a wall through the courtyard.

Cederic pulled her forward. Naveen closed her eyes for an instant, fighting back tears. Shivers ran down her spine. Her head spun. She tried to keep moving, but her body grew weak and her hands trembled. Fear overtook her. Blackness threatened to take hold. She felt someone dragging her by the arms.

Cold. Wet.

She shook her head, seeing color fill back into her vision. Water dripped from her hair. She looked up to see Cederic standing over her, an empty pail in his hands.

"Naveen?" he asked.

"I'm here. What happened?"

She was sitting on the ground. They were no longer outside. Shoes sat on shelves on each wall. They were inside Cederic's business.

"You blacked out before we could reach safety. I had to drag you the rest of the way here."

"Where are the other archers?"

He tilted his head.

"The archers who were following behind us?"

He looked to the ground, away from her.

"Where are they?" she demanded.

"They—they didn't make it."

She stood, her legs wobbling. Cederic grabbed her, keeping her steady. She tried to take a step, but dizziness took over.

"You need to rest," he said.

"We have to help."

"The archers are gone."

"How?" she demanded.

He sighed. "Consumed by fire."

"No ..."

"We cannot fight them, Naveen. They are too strong."

"We have to," she retorted. "If we don't, they'll all land in the city and we're all dead."

He shook his head. "Then we're all dead."

Naveen jerked away from him. She opened the door and gasped. All the streets were blazing in fire. No one was outside.

She scanned the area. Surrounded in fire was a mounted ballista, a massive crossbow aimed toward the sky. It was built to defend against dragons. Naveen glanced to the sky. She saw one dragon, but it was flying away. Gathering up her courage, she bolted out the door.

"Naveen!" Cederic called.

She blocked out his voice. If someone didn't do something, all the dragonriders would land. The city would fall. They would all die. The empire would win. She gritted her teeth. Not if she had anything to say about it.

Her legs carried her as fast as they could. She skidded to a halt at the edge of the flames. The ballista was on the other side. She closed her eyes, concentrated, then shoved her hands forward. Air enveloped her, then exploded forward, brushing the flames to the side to create a small opening. She bolted through it, diving to the ground as the flames closed the gap behind her. Sweat covered her forehead. She panted, trying to catch her breath. Smoke filled her lungs. Tears came to her eyes. She closed them, concentrated, and channeled clean air into her lungs.

Naveen got to her feet. Fatigue tormented her. She pressed on. The ballista was inches away. She checked the massive bolt. It was loaded. Naveen inspected the machine to familiarize herself with its use. She'd seen people practicing with it, but she wished she'd spent time learning how to use it.

A growl filled the air. Chill bumps formed over Naveen's arms. She looked to the sky. The dragon was coming back, and it was looking directly at her. Fear tried to consume her, but she forced it away. She planted her hands on the machine, circling it around to point toward the dragon. She waited. It would need to come closer. But she'd have to release the bolt before it was too close, before it could breathe fire on her. She watched; she waited. The dragon's mouth opened a fraction. It was time.

Naveen checked her aim, then released the massive bolt. It soared into the air. She'd misjudged her target. The bolt was going to miss. It was soaring too high. The dragon's mouth continued to open. Fire would come soon. She'd die here.

Naveen closed her eyes, her lips pressing tightly together. She needed serenity. Air flowed all around her, not as much as normal with all the fire, but it was there. She brought it all to her, as much as she could muster. Her body trembled from the power, from the fatigue.

She opened her eyes, found the ballista's bolt, then threw all of the air at it, redirecting its flight. It adjusted itself, then sprang forward at an even faster speed.

Her eyes widened, mouth dropping open. The dragon's mouth was fully open. The bolt flew inside of it, angling toward the creature's upper jaw. It penetrated all the way, piercing through the top of its head between its eyes. No flames came. The wings ceased flapping; they fell limp. It fell toward the ground.

Naveen was dizzy, exhausted. She fought against it as she watched the dragon crash into the street to the right. The creature skidded on the ground a long ways, its rider falling off in the process.

Naveen tried to hold on for a moment longer, but her strength wouldn't let her. She collapsed onto the ground, holding onto the side of the ballista. Her strength was depleted, and darkness welcomed her.

Chapter 22

Zaviana stepped on the land, wanting with all of her heart to kiss it. She'd thought traveling by ship was rough the first time. However, at least the first time they were traveling at normal speeds. Being blown across an ocean by wind wyverns in a day was terrifying, and sickening. She'd vomited three times during the journey.

Her head still spun as she walked forward. Devarius rushed to her side, keeping her from falling onto the ground.

"Are you all right?" he asked.

She shook her head. "That was a miserable experience."

Zaviana looked around. No one else was experiencing the same feeling as she. People unloaded the ship as if nothing were wrong.

"What is wrong with these people? How are they not as sick as me?" she asked.

Devarius laughed. "Unlike you, we've been riding in ships pushed by wyverns for a while now. We've been conditioning in case it was needed."

Zaviana shook her head. "Well, I guess it's good that you've been conditioning them, because if they all felt like me, we wouldn't reach Saefron for another day."

Pounding footsteps jerked her attention away from her brother. Someone ran toward them. He wore the traditional resistance colors and light leather armor. He panted when he reached them.

"What's wrong?" Devarius asked.

"I'm ..." The man caught his breath. "Glad you've arrived." He panted a few more times before sucking in one large breath. "Dragons are attacking the city."

Devarius cringed. "We're late."

"They haven't been attacking it long. No men have breached the city, but dragons are using fire from above."

Devarius faced Zaviana. "Zavi ... I must go."

"Be safe."

"Always." Devarius kissed her forehead.

He turned to the side, looking to the sky. After a few silent moments, a wyvern appeared, gliding to the ground to land at his side.

He took one last look at Zaviana. "Lead them safely to the city, Zavi. Make sure to stay in the mountains and go around the eastern side to the northern side of the city."

Zaviana frowned. "The gate is on the south side, isn't it?"

He nodded. "It is, and if there's an attack, that's where the empire will be. They will try to breach the gate. However, there is a way inside on the northern side. Lilianya will show you."

Zaviana nodded. "I won't let you down."

"Nor I you, sister."

With that, he climbed atop his wyvern's saddle, and together they flew into the air. More than a hundred wyvernriders followed him.

WIND BRUSHED AGAINST Devarius' face as Ayla carried him swiftly to Saefron. She was still one of the smallest wyverns with a rider, but she was the fastest. They flew high in the air, with a hundred wyverns trailing behind them, resembling a flock of birds in a V formation. Devarius led them northeast, around the eastern side of the city. What would have taken them a full day walking, took less than an hour. He looked down below, noticing a full force of soldiers near the front gate of Saefron. They weren't attacking; they were camping. Fires were ablaze, thousands of warriors surrounding them to stay warm in the harsh winter of the southern mountains. Dragons stayed in the camp as well, but what was most alarming for Devarius were the three dragons circling inside the city. They were spewing flames over the streets. Devarius clenched his teeth.

He angled hard to the right, to lead them away from the camp. Devarius hoped they didn't get too close. He didn't want them to know they'd arrived. They circled around the city, entering it from the northern side. Devarius' mouth dropped when they crossed the southern gate. The entire city was drenched in flames. Several of the buildings, and all of the streets and courtyards, were bathed in it.

Three dragons circled the city, breathing flames onto rooftops as they passed. One dragon flew down toward one of the courtyards. Devarius angled Ayla toward the dragon. With Devarius unable to talk against the heavy wind while in flight, he'd learned how to give Ayla signals for where he wanted to go. When they approached the dragon, Devarius saw a woman at a ballista. His eyes widened when the bolt soared into the air, and then nearly bulged out of their sockets when he saw her use magic to push the bolt into the dragon's open mouth.

How?

The dragon didn't shriek, didn't cry, but it stopped moving and crashed to the ground, its rider falling off during the creature's skid along the flaming roads.

Devarius signaled to the others to fight the two remaining dragons in the city. He led Ayla to the ground to check on the woman.

The dragonrider rose to his feet. He held his left arm against his side. It was limp, and most likely broken. The man unsheathed a dagger and approached the woman at the ballista. Devarius urged Ayla faster. The woman lay on the ground, unconscious.

The dragonrider reached the woman. A malicious grin pasted across his face as he raised the weapon. Devarius wouldn't reach her in time. He turned his head to the side and shouted.

"Ayla!"

He spun his head back around. They were close, but not close enough for Devarius to do anything. Ayla's mouth opened, and a blue streak of fog filled the air in front of her. When the man's dagger was mere inches away from the unconscious woman, his body froze, literally. Blue ice traveled all over his body, freezing him inside.

Devarius landed in front of him. He wrapped his arms around the unconscious woman, dragging her out of the way. Ayla roared into the air, her neck stretching and her voice ear-shattering. Devarius covered his ears as he looked into the sky.

The wyverns defeated the dragons. One of them was falling out of the sky outside of the city, and the last dragon was in full retreat. They'd saved the city. But how many were lost?

"Ayla?"

Yes, little one?

He laughed. "I'm still older than you."

But you're still little.

"Can you do something about all the fire?"

Yes.

Ayla leapt into the sky, flapping her wings to soar above all the flames. Her mouth opened, and blue mist filled her path. The ice turned to water when it hit the flames, and the fire ceased blazing. Several of the other ice wyverns followed Ayla's lead. Fires were put out all over the city. People began to fill the streets.

Devarius saw the resistance's leader, Ellisar, approach.

"You've made it," Ellisar said, a smile spreading across his face.

Devarius' cheeks puffed out. "A little late."

"You did fine. How many came?"

"We have more bringing the crates from the ships, but they won't be here for a day. They're going to have to go around the gate to the northern entrance."

Ellisar nodded. "You best send a few wyvernriders to help protect them."

"Yes. Right now they're just toying with us. We'll need to make sure we're better prepared for their next strike. And we'll need everyone to be successful."

Chapter 23

Naveen's eyes fluttered open. She lay in a room. Her body felt sore. She edged to the end of the bed to sit up. Flashes come to her mind, broken scenes of what happened. Dragons attacking. The city on fire. Her, running through the fire to shoot down a dragon. Blackness. A muscular man with brown skin carrying her. Warmth.

"Naveen? You're awake."

She turned to see the man sitting in the corner of the room. Cederic. Bags were under his eyes, his corneas were cracked with red. He hadn't slept much. Naveen, on the other hand, felt rested.

"Did we survive?" she whispered.

"The wyvernriders came."

Her eyes widened slightly. "Did we win?"

"We fought them out of the city, but no, we didn't win. This doesn't seem like it's going to be a short fight."

She wrinkled her nose. "I was afraid it wouldn't be."

A man stepped into the room. He glanced at the two of them, then smiled. His brown skin glimmered in the torchlight. Muscles bulged through his leather armor. A fire burned inside of the pit of Naveen's stomach. The man was handsome.

He had large lips, a defined chin, green eyes, and close-cropped hair.

"I see you are recovering," he said.

"Yes. Thank you." She paused. "And you are?"

He smiled, sending chills down her spine. "Devarius."

"It's nice to meet you, Devarius."

"Likewise." He grinned.

Devarius strode across the room, passing Cederic, who glared at him with a twisted face, to sit on the edge of the bed next to her.

Chill bumps formed on Naveen's arms.

Devarius frowned at her. "Are you cold?"

"A little," she lied.

It wasn't the cold that gave her shivers. She was quite warm.

"Here," he said. Devarius reached to the bed, grabbing her blanket, and wrapped it around her.

"Thanks." She blushed.

"I saw you."

Naveen tilted her head. "Excuse me?"

"When I arrived with the other wyvernriders, I saw you. No one else was outside. Everyone hid. Except for you. I saw you behind one of the ballistae aiming for a dragon."

Her cheeks reddened even further.

"Why were you out there all alone?"

Cederic's fist clenched in her peripheral vision. His face reddened with anger. Was that directed at her?

"I didn't think you would make it in time to help. I knew if the dragons kept attacking and saw we couldn't fight back—they would bring the rest. They would just land and slaughter us all. I had to do something. I had to show them we could defend ourselves."

Devarius nodded. "You were trying to buy time for us to arrive."

"Yes." Naveen hung her head low. She knew what she did was foolish.

"It could have cost you your life."

"I know," she whispered.

He reached over, cupped her chin, and brought her face up to meet his gaze. "What you did was brave."

Cederic cleared his throat.

Devarius' hand dropped from her face and he smiled. "Do you know, this man here hasn't left your side?"

She glanced to Cederic for only a second before looking back to Devarius. "Are you truly a dragonrider?"

"Wyvernrider."

"What's the difference?" she asked.

He smiled. "Wyverns are a lot smaller than dragons. And they only have two legs."

"Oh," she said, a touch of disappointment in her tone.

"But," Devarius reassured her, "they're a lot swifter, and the ones with us breathe a lot more than fire."

"Really?" she asked.

"Yes. There—"

"Do you have a purple wyvern with you?"

Devarius blinked several times before answering. "Yes, several. Most people don't know dragons or wyverns have more than one color. Tell me ... what makes you ask about a purple wyvern?"

She reached under her garments and revealed her necklace. A shimmering dragonscale glimmered against the torchlight.

"Is that a—"

"A dragonscale. Or, I guess it could be a wyvernscale."

Devarius gently grabbed the scale and inspected it closer. After turning it around several times, he let it drop then looked into her eyes. "I saw you push that ballista bolt through the air."

"Tell me ..." Naveen whispered, "what abilities do the purple wyvern have?"

"Hmm?" he asked.

"You said the wyverns with you do more than breathe fire. Do the purple wyverns breathe fire?"

He shook his head. "No, they have strong breath."

"They control the wind."

"Yes, in a manner of speaking."

She clutched the necklace tight.

"What is it?" he asked.

She took a deep breath before answering. "With this scale, I can control the wind around me. I can feel it, each molecule. I can call to it, bring it to me, then release it."

"You believe it's the scale, and not an inner ability?"

"There's another."

"Someone else can channel the wind?" he asked.

"No. He has a red scale."

Devarius' eyes bulged. "He can channel fire?"

She nodded.

"If it is truly the scales ..." Devarius muttered.

"What?" she asked.

"We have a dragon's carcass rotting in the courtyard right now. We can arm everyone with a scale."

Naveen grinned.

"Are you feeling well?" he asked.

"Yes. Why?"

"I would like you to accompany a few of the wyvernriders to make sure the path is safe for my sister and the rest of our companions."

"Your sister?"

"Zaviana."

Naveen's eyes widened. "Zaviana is your sister?"

"You know her?" he asked.

"She's the one who helped us and brought us here."

He smiled. "Will you help then?"

She wrinkled her nose. "Why me?"

He looked away, his cheeks darkening. "I believe your abilities may be useful to aid the others."

She nodded, understanding. "If I can help, I will."

"Meet me in the courtyard after you get ready."

She nodded. "I will."

Devarius stood, nodded to her and Cederic, then departed the room.

Cederic stood. "Are you sure about this?"

Naveen frowned. "What's to be unsure of?"

"It's dangerous out there."

"It's also dangerous in here. No matter where we go right now, the Dragonia Empire will follow. People need my help. I will not turn my back on them."

He huffed. "Just ... be safe, all right?"

"I will."

He leaned in, grabbed her in a hug, then released her and walked out the door.

Naveen smiled after him.

After getting dressed in her leather armor and making sure she secured her sword to her belt, she stepped outside. She didn't know what she expected, but what she saw took her breath away.

The fires were all gone, replaced with snow-covered grounds. People practiced archery and sword fighting in the courtyard. Others roamed the streets, laughing and talking to each other. It looked completely different. Saefron was no longer a dead city. It was bursting with activity, with hope. She saw wyverns everywhere. Several walked along the ground, but others were flying in the sky. She glanced up and saw hundreds of them flying over the city. At first, she was scared, thinking they were dragons, but she remembered what Devarius had told her. All the creatures above the city had only two legs. She continued walking forward to the courtyard.

When she neared her first wyvern, she inspected the creature. It was a third the size of a dragon, if not a little smaller. She held out a hand. The wyvern tilted its head, bent down, sniffed her hand, then licked it.

She laughed.

"There you are," Devarius called.

Naveen smiled at his approach.

"I want you to meet my good friend, Paedyn. He will be leading the retrieval party."

Paedyn, a handsome pale man, stepped forward. He had short dark blond hair, long eyelashes, and thick lips. A smile came across his face as he bowed to her.

"Nice to meet you," she said.

He grabbed her hand and kissed it. "The pleasure is mine."

"All right, Paedyn, go easy on her. You have a mission to complete."

Paedyn raised his brows at Devarius. "All right, are you ready?"

He pointed to a large red wyvern.

"Ready for what?"

"Well, we can't exactly walk there. We'll have to fly."

Naveen's eyes bulged. "Fly?"

Paedyn laughed. "Don't worry, you won't have to fly alone. You'll be riding with me."

"I will?"

Paedyn grinned. "Yes. I suggest you hold on tight."

Naveen gulped.

Chapter 24

Zaviana and Lilianya led all the warriors into the mountains. They were careful to scout ahead to make sure they wouldn't run into the empire. Zaviana had a good memory, but they were going a different way into Saefron, and she relied on Lilianya's guidance for directions.

The crates slowed them down significantly. Devarius had been smart enough to not make the crates too long, making a single man able to carry one, but with over thirty crates of wyvern oil, it was a slow process. Especially since the oil was so fragile that if a single vial was dropped and its contents spilled, it could be catastrophic for everyone.

After hours of relentless traveling, they arrived on the eastern side of Saefron. They were still a ways out, since they had to travel far through the mountains to the east to avoid the empire gathered on the southern border of the city. They still had to reach the northern side of Saefron.

Lilianya had them stop to take a break. Zaviana checked on all the men, including the valuable crates. Before she could finish her inspection, clanging metal echoed in the distance. A raiding party of over a hundred empire warriors charged them. Zaviana unsheathed her sword. The warriors with them drew their weapons, though they weren't as prepared to battle, and many were fatigued. Women who weren't warriors ran to the center to the protection of the warriors. Zaviana's blade met a warrior's. He slammed his sword to her left, then right before pulling back and slamming an overhead strike. Zaviana spun out of the way, grabbed a dagger from her belt, and threw it into the attacker's neck. The man collapsed to the ground.

Another man approached; he wielded a spiked ball mace instead of a sword. His attacks were harder to fight against. Her sword rolled over the spherical weapon several times. Even though the length of his weapon was shorter, its bluntness made it a much stronger weapon than her sword. When he slammed the mace toward her, and she intercepted it with her sword, vibrations tore through her entire body, causing her to stagger and drop to the ground. The man pounced on top of her, slamming his weapon down. She rolled out of the way, but the tip of one of the spikes tore into her armor and scratched along her right shoulder. Zaviana stood, fell backward slightly, then felt her shoulder. Blood smeared across her hand. She gritted her teeth.

Looking to her left and right, she noticed no more warriors were there to fight her, so she paused and channeled the energy around her. She focused it to the warrior, whose eyes widened in fear as flames spiraled at him. He shrieked. Zaviana stepped forward, stabbing her sword through his chest.

She took a step back and looked at the scene before her. Several of the men and women warriors with her had fallen, but so had many of the empire soldiers. They outnumbered the empire three to one, but several of their company weren't warriors. They'd needed blacksmiths, leatherworkers, and several other tradesmen to come with them to help make materials to fight back.

Zaviana did a quick count and noticed less than thirty opponents remained. They could do this. She stepped forward, feeling the energy all around her, all the particles floating in the air. Her hand moved forward, a blue glow surrounding it. Warriors stopped what they were doing to watch her. Several of them broke ranks to charge her. She released the energy. A glow arched like a rainbow from her palm, separating like lightning as it touched each of her opponents. When the blue energy touched them, they froze inside a thin layer of ice.

Five men stood frozen in ice in front of Zaviana. She charged them, slicing her sword against each one to shatter them into pieces. After she was done, she inspected the surrounding area, expecting more men to come her way. None did. The remaining men who weren't engaged in battle turned around and fled.

"Fight!" Zaviana called. "Stop them!"

Her allies charged after some of the men, and others were stopped with arrows. Zaviana blasted a few with a yellow energy, which turned into lightning as it struck them. They stopped most of the men, but one escaped. Zaviana ran after him, but he was too far away, and he disappeared through a mountain pass. She fell to her knees, sheathing her sword and running her fingers through her long black hair.

Lilianya walked over to her. "Zaviana?"

"One of them escaped."

"It's fine. We defeated most of them."

Zaviana shook her head. "No, he will warn the others. They will come. We can fight a small skirmish, but what can we do against a few dragonriders?"

Lilianya's eyes widened. "We need to go."

Zaviana nodded. "And we need to hurry."

Chapter 25

Paedyn spotted Zaviana and the others on the eastern side of Saefron. They weren't close to the city, but on the other side of a meadow, approaching the city from a distance. Smart. He motioned to the five other wyvernriders behind him, and they began to descend. Naveen gripped him tighter. He smiled. A bug flew into his mouth. Paedyn gagged.

When they reached land, a decent ways ahead of the party, Paedyn climbed off Pyro and headed toward them, a hand waving in the air. At first, they were cautious approaching, but soon they pressed forward excitedly.

"Thank the Creator you're here," Lilianya said when she approached.

Paedyn raised his eyebrows. "I knew you missed me."

Lilianya rolled her eyes. "You wish."

"Every shooting star," he replied.

Naveen turned to him, then looked at Lilianya. "Is he always like this?"

Lilianya's lips pressed together as she shook her head. "Sadly ... yes. You know, if he wasn't so arrogant, he might be all right."

"Did you just say I am handsome?" Paedyn asked.

"No," Lilianya said.

His eyebrows lifted and fell several times. "I think you did. I just can't help it. Every one wants to be with me."

Lilianya rolled her eyes.

"How is everyone doing?"

"We were attacked," Zaviana said as she approached.

Paedyn's eyes grew wide. "Is everyone all right?"

"We lost fifteen."

His mouth twisted with distaste.

"One of them escaped."

Paedyn stared blankly at her.

"He's most likely warning the others to come find us."

"Right. Dragonriders. We don't like dragonriders. Is everyone ready?" he asked.

"Where are we going?" Zaviana asked.

"North," Paedyn responded.

Zaviana rolled her eyes.

"Follow me," Paedyn said.

He turned around and led them further north. His wyvern, Pyro, walked along at his side. The other five wyvernriders were dismounted with their wyverns following on foot. They traveled through the forest. The sun began to fall into the western horizon as snow started to fall.

"More snow," Zaviana muttered.

"Fear not, snow is our ally."

"Ally?" she asked.

He smiled as she stepped to walk by his side. Paedyn hadn't realized how attractive Devarius' sister was. He wondered if they truly were siblings. Devarius didn't look that good. His face was rough, leathery, with a bit of wrinkles when he smiled

and raised his brows with excitement. His sister, howe
smooth dark brown skin, the same color as an oak tr
hair fell past her shoulders, straight, and gleamed under the
light of the sunset. Zaviana's lips were, well, large and moist.
Shivers traveled up Paedyn's spine. This was his friend's sister.
He shouldn't look at her that way. Her hazelnut-color eyes
should have no place in their mission. Was that a freckle in the
right one? He shook his head. What did she ask?

"Hazelnut?" Paedyn asked.

"Excuse me?"

"I like hazelnuts. They're delicious. Have you ever tried
one?"

Her eyebrows wrinkled. "What does that have to do with
snow?"

"Oh. Sorry. For some reason I started thinking about hazelnuts. I can't recall why."

She rolled her eyes.

Everyone rolled their eyes at Paedyn. He always liked
watching the color make a circle, exposing the white sclera. It
always fascinated him. Most people rolled their eyes from top
to left and around, but a few did it the other way. He wondered
why.

"As I was saying," Paedyn said, "the snow is our ally. It will
cover our tracks."

Zaviana inhaled, then blew loudly out her nose. "I suppose."

"But seriously, have you ever tried a hazelnut?"

Her eyes widened as she looked at him. "I can't recall."

He grinned. "Well, perhaps I'll have to get you to try some. You know, they have some at the pub in Saefron. Perhaps we could go tonight."

Her mouth parted. "Are you being serious right now?"

"Umm ... no?"

"Good, because we are being attacked by who knows how many dragons and the entire empire. The last thing I care about are nuts."

Paedyn shrugged. "I care."

As they reached the southern side of the city, Paedyn thought they were home free. Or Saefron free. Close enough to slip in. Whatever. He thought they would be fine; he was wrong. Three dragons dropped out of the sky.

Paedyn's mouth opened, exposing his teeth, and his eyes wrinkled around the sides.

"One, two, three. Yup. There are three of them," Paedyn said.

Zaviana stopped, one hand on the hilt of her sword, the other held in front of her, a strange glow emanating from her fingers.

Paedyn closed his mouth and pursed his lips as he watched her. "That is neat."

Her eyes grew wide as her head stretched forward. He followed her gaze.

"Oh, right." He turned to face the three dragonriders. "Good evening. I don't suppose you want to surrender?"

One of the dragons roared.

Paedyn's shoulders stretched to his head. "Worth a try."

Are you done playing games? I'm ready to flame, Pyro said in his mind.

"I like flames," Paedyn said.

Everyone looked at him strangely. He walked forward, unsheathing his sword. The three dragonriders stared at him with disbelief. He twirled the blade in his hands, making the blade shift from his left to his right.

One of the dragons opened its mouth, growling as it prepared to release its fire. Paedyn grinned, grabbed a glass vial from his belt, and threw it toward the dragon. He dove to his right as the dragon's flames erupted from its throat.

Before the flames could reach far, they shattered the vial, exploding a few ounces of fire oil a few feet from the three dragonriders. Flames erupted in the air, a loud bang shook the snow around them, and the three dragonriders blasted backward. One of the riders lay dead in a mountain of flames. His dragon was injured, one of its wings shattered.

"Now, Pyro!"

His wyvern flew forward. Paedyn leapt into the air. Pyro flew underneath him. He landed on his dragon, grabbing the reins as he passed. Paedyn began laughing maniacally as they flew into the sky.

"That was a lot of flames, Pyro!" he shouted.

That was foolish, Pyro said.

"Foolishly brilliant!" Paedyn grinned. "I bet you can't make that many flames."

Bet on.

They flew toward the injured dragon, Pyro blazing fire toward the creature. Fire didn't hurt the dragons as much as the other elements, but it still did damage.

"I don't know, Pyro. Yours didn't go bang."

Give me one of your vials. I'll make a bang.

Paedyn clicked his tongue in his mouth. "Now, now. These vials are mine."

Technically, they're mine.

"What you're referring to is the oil inside. However, the vials, the glass, yup, they're totally mine."

They circled back around the injured dragon. Paedyn flung a vial at the creature. Pyro didn't hesitate. Flames erupted from the wyvern's mouth, catching the vial as it nearly reached the injured dragon. Another loud bang echoed as the vial exploded into a massive burst of flame. The flames consumed the dragon, and the large beast collapsed to the ground, black instead of its natural red hue.

The other five wyvernriders with him, two blue, two gold, and one purple, flew around the remaining two dragonriders. They used their elements to attack, but the two dragons were smarter than the first.

"It looks like they could use a distraction," Paedyn said.

What did you have in mind?

"How long can you breathe fire? Can we make rings of fire around the two dragons?"

Not wide.

Paedyn grinned. "Thin is fine."

They flew toward the two dragons. Paedyn rubbed Pyro's neck as he held onto the reins with his left hand. The reins were more for helping the rider stay on than directing the wyvern, though in times of need where speech was impossible, it did help. When they were close enough, Paedyn flicked the reins, signaling Pyro to begin their crazy plan. Flames filled the air below them in a thin line. They circled the dragons three times, making three thin lines of flame around them. Both dragons turned to face them, mouths stretching wide and flames heading straight for them.

"Away, Pyro!"

The wyvern tried to turn, but the flames caught them on Pyro's underside. Paedyn hung onto the reins tight as Pyro spun in circles and they headed toward the ground. He closed his eyes, not wanting to see the world spinning around him anymore. It didn't help. Dizziness still consumed him. Blackness found him.

Chapter 26

Zaviana dove out of the way as Paedyn and his wyvern tumbled toward her. She stood, brushed herself off, then turned to look at Paedyn. He was still atop his wyvern, but he wasn't moving. She slowly stepped toward him. The wyvern opened its eyes and groaned. Zaviana reached Paedyn. He was slumped forward in his saddle with his eyes closed. Zaviana checked his pulse. He was alive.

The wyvern tried to stand, grumbling all the while.

"Are you all right?" Zaviana asked.

The wyvern stared at her, then nodded.

"Well, your rider isn't. He needs to rest."

The wyvern turned to look at Paedyn, looked back to Zaviana, then shook its head.

"You want to go back and fight?"

Yes, a voice projected inside Zaviana's mind.

She jumped, not expecting the cracked voice.

"Would you mind if I ride you?"

The wyvern tilted its head, then moved it around as if inspecting Zaviana.

Zaviana approached the wyvern. It took one step backward, but Zaviana didn't go toward its head. She reached the creature's back, unstrapped Paedyn, and eased him to the ground. Instead of waiting for the wyvern to decide, she climbed atop the saddle, secured herself, petted the wyvern's neck, and whispered, "Let's go."

The wyvern swayed its neck, as if unsure what to do, and was surprised by Zaviana's forwardness. After a second of deliberation, the creature crouched, then leapt into the air.

Zaviana gripped the reins tighter as they soared into the air. Wind brushed against her face, tossing her long hair behind her head. It hurt. She'd have to remember to tie her hair back next time. Next time? Did she dare do this again? It was exhilarating being in the sky, feeling the momentum of the wyvern's flight. She looked down. Zaviana gulped. She shouldn't have done that. Her eyes closed as she positioned her head upward. When her eyes opened, she realized they were close to the opposing dragons. One of them was injured. She angled the reins to focus the wyvern on the injured one. Zaviana hoped they had been trained similar to horses, because horses were all she knew.

"What is your name?" Zaviana yelled, wind catching in her mouth, making her gag.

Pyro, the creature responded in her mind.

A large flame shot from the creature's mouth, arching toward the dragon. It hit directly on the creature's head as it was turned to snap at a smaller blue wyvern. The fire hurt the wyvern, but not as much as Zaviana thought it would. She wrinkled her nose.

Zaviana covered her mouth with her hand as she screamed, "Take me closer."

Pyro's head spun around to look at her. The wyvern didn't have a facial expression like a human, but Zaviana could have sworn its eyes grew slightly larger, as if asking her if she were serious. Zaviana nodded.

Pyro's head shook, but she continued toward the dragon. Zaviana closed her eyes. There was much energy in the sky. She could feel moisture all around her in the air, in the clouds. Zaviana channeled it all to her. The air all around them grew dry, all its humidity drained. Zaviana compressed cold next, forming a sheet of cold air in front of the moisture she'd collected. She opened her eyes. They were close to the dragon now. Zaviana released the energy. Water spouted forward, through the sheet of cold, and transformed into liquid ice as it covered the dragon.

The dragon's red body turned blue, then ice collected on its hide until it was several inches thick. Ice covered the rider and the dragon's wings last. It couldn't flap its wings to stay afloat anymore. A piercing shriek left its throat, shattering the ice from its jaw as it tumbled toward the ground.

Zaviana finally looked down again, watching as the dragon crashed into the snowy earth and shattered into a thousand pieces.

Brilliant, Pyro said.

"Thank you," Zaviana whispered.

They circled around the empty space where the dragon had just been, and along with the other two wyvernriders, they approached the last dragon. Elements blazed through the air: Pyro's fire, the two ice wyverns' ice, and lightning from the two gold wyverns. The purple wind wyvern stood on the ground recovering from a minor injury. Zaviana began to channel more moisture from the air, but it wasn't as strong this time. She was weaker, her fatigue growing. When she released, it was only as powerful as the ice wyverns. It connected with a wing, partially freezing it and making it difficult for the dragon to remain in the air.

The dragon roared, blowing fire all around it. All the wyvernriders flew away to avoid the flames. When Pyro flew back around to find the dragon, they saw him using his own flames to melt the ice off of his wing. The dragon roared one last time, then flew away, escaping toward the empire's camp.

"We did it," she breathed, a smile creeping onto her face.

Pyro landed in front of the party along with the other five wyverns. Zaviana slid off the wyvern, then nearly fell forward when she tried to walk. Her inner thighs ached. It'd been a long time since she'd ridden a horse, and a wyvern was a little bit wider than the horses she'd ridden.

You did well, little one, Pyro said.

"As did you, Pyro," she said.

Paedyn stumbled over. "You stole my wyvern."

"Borrowed." Zaviana smiled.

I am no one's property, Pyro said.

"You totally are. We talked about this, Pyro. You're my fire. Without you I don't have fire. I need fire in my life. Therefore, you are mine, and I am yours. End of story."

Paedy— the wyvern tried to speak.

"I said, end of story!"

Zaviana laughed.

Paedyn wrinkled his nose. "Is he projecting to you too?"

She nodded.

Paedyn shook his head. "Now you're even talking to other people. I am hurt. Do you hear me, Pyro! Hurt."

The wyvern tilted her head down to try and touch her nose against Paedyn.

"No! Don't touch me. I'm going to be mad at you for the next five minutes. You'll have to wait."

A soft chortling noise came from the wyvern's throat.

"Don't laugh at me! Six minutes!" He stormed off.

"Is he serious?" Zaviana asked.

Mostly, no. He is rather attached to me. I call him my pet human, Pyro said.

Zaviana stifled a laugh.

Lilianya approached. "We need to leave."

Zaviana nodded her head. "Yes, we don't want that remaining dragonrider to bring more to us before we can get to safety." She brushed her hair down over her shoulders with her fingers. Her hair hurt. "How much longer?"

"Not long. Follow me," Lilianya said.

Chapter 27

Devarius saw Paedyn's signal on the southern side of the city. It wasn't hard to miss. Paedyn wasn't exactly a surreptitious kind of guy. Flames burned in the air on the southern side reading, "Boo."

Shaking his head, Devarius strode over to the hidden entrance. He brushed hay aside to reveal a small tunnel, large enough for men and women to climb through, but too small for a wyvern or dragon. It was meant to be an escape route, but they hadn't forseen this many coming to attack at once. They would only die in the cold of the mountains in the winter if everyone left through it.

He stood over the hole. Over four inches of ice blocked it from entry. Devarius motioned over a fire wyvern. The creature nodded at Devarius, then blazed fire onto the ice. It was thick enough to take several long minutes before it completely melted. Paedyn would need to do the same thing outside the city.

After several long minutes, people started climbing into the city. Devarius stood at the entrance to help everyone up. Once everyone was safe, and they made a few checks to make sure no one was left behind, Devarius had Ayla breathe ice back over the entrance, securing it.

Devarius hugged his sister. "I'm glad you made it back safe."

"We lost a few," she admitted.

Devarius raised a brow. "You were attacked?"

"A small party of a hundred warriors attacked us on the eastern side. We defeated them, but we lost a few. Shortly after, your friend, Paedyn, found us and brought us to the southern side."

Devarius glanced at Paedyn. "Good."

"There, we fought against three dragonriders. But we defeated them as well."

"Dragonriders attacked on the eastern side?"

He turned to Paedyn. "You did make sure to cover the entrance well?"

"Of course. I even melted a gigantic rock on top of it," Paedyn responded.

"Good. Did you lose anyone to the dragons?"

Paedyn shook his head. "No, but your sister stole my wyvern."

"What?" Devarius asked.

"Borrowed," Zaviana said.

Paedyn rolled his eyes. "Borrow implies asking."

"I did ask, you were just unconscious."

"Do I need to put you two in time-out?" Devarius asked.

Zaviana smiled.

Paedyn frowned.

Devarius laughed. "Come on, we need to prepare the defenses. If we live through this attack, we can sort out the semantics."

They turned to watch all the crates being brought into an empty forge. The men were careful when they carried them, sweat beading along their faces, even with the cold.

"Do those crates weigh that much?" Zaviana asked.

Devarius shook his head. "They're just nervous. If one of the vials breaks ... well, it won't be good for any of us."

"What do you plan on doing with them?" Zaviana asked.

Devarius shrugged. "I haven't had time to experiment with them."

"I make them go boom," Paedyn said.

Zaviana rolled her eyes. "I saw what you did with them. There has to be more practical ways to use them."

"All I know is it seemed important enough to save the oil. I am unsure what all we can do with it. The only way we've used it is throwing them at a target."

"Didn't you say one small drop is highly effective?"

Devarius nodded. "One small drop of fire oil makes a large bonfire. One small drop of ice will freeze a rat solid."

"How many drops are in each vial?"

Devarius furrowed his eyebrows. "How should I know?"

Zaviana shook her head. "How much of this precious oil are you wasting?"

"Excuse me," Paedyn cut in. "But our elegant approach has been working just fine, thank you."

"Elegant? Throwing full vials of oil at dragons?"

Paedyn nodded. "Yes. As I said, elegant."

Zaviana shook her head. "And what happens when you throw one of these vials inside the city, and it misses?"

Paedyn wrinkled his nose. "Pray?"

Zaviana snorted. "Have you tried using the oil on arrows?"

Devarius raised a brow. "Arrows?"

"Arrows by themselves are useless against a dragon, but if covered in ice oil, or lightning, what effect might they have?"

Devarius' eyes bulged. "That's brilliant."

Paedyn crossed his arms. "You're just saying that because she's your sister."

"And what about the large ballistae? We can put oil on the larger bolts as well," Zaviana said.

Paedyn scratched his chin. "Wait a minute. How are you going to fit a bolt in a vial? The bolt is way too big."

Zaviana closed her eyes, took a deep breath, and resisted the urge to slap him. "Put the oil in jars. Scatter the jars through the city, in places least likely for a direct hit with dragonfire."

Devarius nodded. "Find us some jars, Paedyn."

"As you wish," he grumbled, walking away.

"Does he not like me?" Zaviana asked.

Devarius shook his head. "Don't worry about him. He's mostly joking. However, I think you proving you could ride his wyvern as good as him is what irritated him. He'll get over it."

"I hope so."

"What else do you recommend, Zavi?"

"It looks like several of the mounted ballistae were damaged. We should make repairs and check to make sure they're adjusted properly."

Devarius nodded. "Come, let us get to work."

The two of them walked through the city together, checking all the jars that had been strategically placed by Paedyn and the archers, as well as the improvements on the ballistae. They worked for hours to make sure everything was secure and lids were secured on all the oil jars.

As sunset approached, a light snow began to fall. It sizzled against the torches inside the city and aggravated most of the men and women who worked hard at securing the city's defense. Devarius looked up into the sky. Wyverns circled the skies, at least a dozen of them, patrolling. As the snow picked up, a white haze blocked out the view, until the wyverns were hard to see.

Devarius took a deep breath, then looked away. Ellisar approached him. At his side walked a dragon. Devarius' hand touched the hilt of his sword.

"Ayla," he called.

Ayla didn't respond, but in less than a minute, she landed by his side. A low grumble echoed in her throat.

Ellisar held his hands up, and the dragon at his side stopped walking forward. "Easy now, Devarius."

"What is this?" Devarius snapped.

"Her name is Alora, and she is a friend."

"She is a dragon ..."

"Yes, she is. And she is loyal to me," Ellisar said.

"How long have you had this dragon?" Devarius asked.

"She has been my friend for over eighty-six years."

Zaviana stepped next to her brother. Her mouth fell open. "Eighty-six years?"

"Yes."

"How is that possible?" Devarius asked.

"When a man bonds to a dragon, perhaps even a wyvern, I'm not sure, they are connected. Humans don't live to a hundred, at least, not often. Dragons, however, live for hundreds of years. They aren't immortal, but I believe some have made it to over a thousand."

"A thousand years?" Zaviana asked.

Ellisar nodded.

"And how did you get this dragon?"

Ellisar took a deep breath. "Galedar and I were friends long ago. Most people don't know this, but the emperor is over a hundred years old as well. Not a lot of the empire actually meets him. He stays hidden in the shadows, in his rooms, and hardly steps outside."

Devarius' eyebrows rose. "You were friends with the emperor?"

"He wasn't always corrupt. In the beginning, all he wanted was peace. We grew up in a time before people knew of dragons. There was no empire. All we had were small regions, with dukes and earls fighting over territories. It was constant battling, human against human. Galedar wanted to change that."

Devarius ran his hand over his short hair. "And he thought uniting everyone under one banner would do that?"

Ellisar nodded. "And it did, for a time. However, peace was strange for humans. Many of the dukes and earls had been thrown out, but new people tried to step up to take their place. It was a constant battle to keep everyone peaceful. We realized the peaceful tactics of unity wasn't working."

"So you turned to tyranny?" Devarius glared at Ellisar.

Ellisar frowned. "He did. I did not know at first. The new leaders of the cities who were fighting against the unity began disappearing, and I began to question Galedar. He assured me everything was fine."

"He lied," Zaviana said.

Ellisar nodded. "Yes. I began to listen to the whispers. People were becoming afraid of us, afraid of him. He brought more

dragons from Dragonia and found power-hungry r
began his climb to power and tyranny."

"So you left?" Devarius asked.

Ellisar shook his head. "No. I tried to reason with him at first. We got into several arguments. He would not listen. Then, a meteor struck the land. We went to investigate. He dared not get too close, but sent another rider in. The rider's dragon touched the stone, and his intelligence left him."

Devarius tilted his head. "His intelligence?"

"Yes," Ellisar said. "Dragons were once intelligent like the wyverns are now. They used to communicate with us. Something happened when that dragon touched the meteor. His essence and intelligence disappeared in a swirl of red smoke and was absorbed into the strange rock. Now, the dragons are nothing more than wild beasts."

Devarius' mouth was open wide. "Is your dragon?"

Ellisar smiled. "We left before he could get to her. He began making orders for all the dragonriders to meet with him. That's when he forced all the dragons to touch the stone. I realized he'd changed. He no longer sought peace, but power. I left, never to look back. Instead, I worked on building a force to challenge him, to fight against the empire. I want to bring peace to this land. Tyranny was never my goal."

Devarius glanced to the dragon by Ellisar's side. The creature wasn't red like the other dragons he'd seen. He was a dark blue. Devarius hadn't paid attention before. All he'd seen was a massive dragon.

"Your dragon ... it isn't like the others." Devarius paused. "She's an ice dragon, isn't she?"

Ellisar grinned. "Yes. She is the only ice dragon."

Zaviana shook her head. "No, there is another."

Ellisar raised his eyebrows.

"Derkas has one."

"The mercenary?" Devarius asked.

Zaviana nodded. "It was his payment for returning the man who was coming to find you with information on the dragon stone all those years ago."

"Strange. There weren't supposed to be any others."

"From what Derkas told me, it was an egg, and it hatched for him."

Surprise showed on Ellisar's face. "Is that so?"

"Why did you say there weren't supposed to be any others?" Devarius asked.

"This is mostly speculation. But as far as I could gather, the fire dragons were the ones Galedar found. They were the ones who rallied to him. Several of the others saw what he was doing and left Dragonia. A few of their eggs remained, which is how I found Alora here. But once Galedar became tyrannical, Alora sent a message to the rest of the blue dragons, including the eggs, to never hatch for the emperor. I believe the other dragon eggs left behind of different colors had similar messages from their parents. Dragons can live inside the protection of their eggs for thousands of years if they desire."

"Perhaps Derkas' dragon sensed something about him worth hatching for," Zaviana said.

"You're not still hung up on that mercenary, are you?" Devarius asked.

"He did save my life ... twice. He has a kind heart, even if he refuses to admit it."

Devarius rolled his eyes.

Silence filled the air for several long moments.

Devarius coughed. "So, what now?"

Ellisar shrugged. "Now, we fight. The time has come for me to expose myself. The time has come for Alora to make her presence known. We need to save Saefron and continue building an army of wyvernriders. Eventually, we'll be able to fight the empire, but for right now, we need to survive."

Devarius nodded. "Agreed."

Chapter 28

Two days passed with little happening. The Dragonia Empire camped outside the gate, and the resistance continued building and checking their defenses. Wyverns patrolled the skies above the city, but no attack came. It was a stalemate.

Several of them sat at a table inside the meeting room discussing what options they had. They were hopeful the dragonscales they'd carved off the hide of the dragon would prove useful, but no one besides Naveen and Fraeyn had been able to get them to work yet. They hadn't given up on them, but knew they needed a backup plan in case they didn't work.

Devarius stretched. "Do you think they're trying to box us in here and starve us?"

Paedyn shook his head. "Not likely. If they think we don't have supplies to last a few winters, they're sorely mistaken."

Devarius snorted with a small nod. "Yes. When you're hiding from the empire, that's one thing you make sure you have ... supplies."

"What will we do once this is over?" Paedyn asked.

"You mean, if we survive?"

"Of course we'll survive. We can't let a good-looking man like me go to waste."

Devarius shook his head. "We'll have to abandon this city."

"I know. Where will we go? Adeth Isle?"

Devarius nodded. "I believe that was always the plan. If you noticed, Ellisar kept leading us there since I found it. More and more warriors were sent there. We've been building the island larger and larger. We're not quite ready for this many people, but we could handle it."

Paedyn nodded.

A shriek echoed through the building. Screaming came next.

Devarius stood, his hand touching the hilt of his sword.

"What's that?" Paedyn asked.

"I don't know ... come on."

Devarius burst out the door. A woman lay dead on the street in a pool of her own blood. Devarius glanced around, but saw nothing. Several women and men were running away from the scene. Their expressions were blank, their faces white, eyes bulged. They looked like they'd seen a ghost. The people were horrified.

Devarius held his sword steady. A blur rushed in front of him, and he began wavering his weapon slightly in front of him as his eyes attempted to focus. Still, he could see nothing. Paedyn stood by his left side, his rapier held firm.

"What's going on?" Devarius called.

No one paid him any heed. They continued to run away, slipping into buildings.

Devarius walked forward. Paedyn stayed by his side. A woman stood in the courtyard hanging laundry. She hadn't run with the others. It didn't seem she even knew of the danger. Devarius began to approach her. Before he reached her, a dagger penetrated through her bosom from her back.

Devarius rushed forward. The woman crumpled to the ground. He saw a shadow disappear from behind her.

"What in the blazing thorns?" Paedyn asked as he skidded to a halt next to Devarius.

"The shadow!" Devarius yelled.

A shadow ran across the courtyard toward more people.

"What?" Paedyn asked.

"There is a shadow, look!" Devarius pointed.

"What in the blazes is casting the shadow? There's no one there!"

"I know," Devarius snarled. "Come on."

Devarius sprinted toward the shadow. Most of the courtyard erupted in chaos, women and children screaming as they ran to their homes. A few men littered the area, most of them with swords held in front of them, searching for the threat. The shadow dodged one of the men, slipping behind him, then a knife appeared in front of the man's throat, slitting it all the way across.

The man gurgled as he collapsed to the ground. A warrior next to the fallen man began swinging his sword sporadically, not knowing where the threat was. The shadow dodged the swings from left to right, blocking a few of the strikes with a shadow sword. When metal clanged against metal, the warrior gasped, stepping backward. He continued swinging his weapon, but its pattern became even worse.

Devarius nearly reached the man, but before he could, the shadow dove out of the way, kicking the backside of the warrior's legs. When the warrior fell, the shadow was on its knees, slamming its weapon into the throat of the man.

Paedyn leapt toward the shadow, slashing his weapon furiously. Devarius stepped by his side, and the two of them fought against the shadow man. His image was distorted, much like an actual shadow, making his attacks hard to predict. Devarius finally broke through his defenses, stabbing his sword through the shadow's heart.

The shadow collapsed to the ground, its entire body seizing. A man appeared, then disappeared abruptly, transforming back into a shadow. The body continued to change between a shadow and a man for several long minutes before he stopped moving completely and turned fully back into a human.

"What was that?" Paedyn asked.

"I don't know," Devarius responded.

The streets crowded with people once more. With the threat being dead, men gathered the bodies of the fallen, and many crowded around Devarius and Paedyn, asking them what had happened.

Thick, dark red blood oozed out of the shadow man's mouth, unlike any blood Devarius had ever seen before. Some of the man's skin was darkened black in spots.

"How did he get inside the city?" Zaviana asked from behind them.

Devarius turned around to look at his sister. "I don't know. He was a shadow. The whole fight, and every one he killed, he was only a shadow. It was almost impossible to see him."

"A shadow?" she asked.

Devarius nodded. "Yes ... like an actual shadow."

Her eyes widened. "If they can make their people into shadows ..."

Devarius gulped.

"We're going to need more fire," Paedyn said.

"We need to investigate this," Zaviana said.

"I agree," Devarius said.

Zaviana spun around and began to walk away.

"Where are you going?" Devarius asked.

"I told you, we need to investigate this."

His eyes widened as his chin lowered, wrinkles forming on his forehead. "And you think you're going to be the one to do it?"

She shrugged. "Someone has to."

He shook his head. "Not you."

"And why not?"

"I just got you back, Zavi. I'm not going to lose you again."

She clenched her teeth. "I can take care of myself."

Devarius tilted his head. "And what is your plan? Are you just going to stalk over there and ask them how they make men into shadows?"

She wrinkled her nose. "No, I was just going to spy on them."

"I said no," Devarius said.

"And who put you in charge?"

"Ellisar put me in charge, and I'm telling you no. You are too important to lose. I will not let you go out there. We can find another way."

"I will go," a voice whispered.

Devarius raised a brow at the young woman who approached them. Naveen. His lips pressed tightly together. He didn't want any woman to go out alone when there were thousands of cruel warriors with the Dragonia Empire outside.

"Are you sure, Naveen?" Zaviana asked.

She nodded. "I've been looking for a way I can help."

"You've helped enough. You shot down a dragon and helped retrieve Zaviana," Devarius said.

Zaviana glared at Devarius. "We need someone to check on what's going on. We've both seen how capable Naveen is. Are you going to reject her too?"

"I—"

"Is this because we're women? Do you think we need a big strong man to take care of us? Because I assure you, we're more than capable."

"It's not that," he pleaded.

"Oh really? Then what is it?"

Devarius hung his head, defeated. "Naveen, it is dangerous to go out there. Are you sure?"

Naveen nodded. "Yes. I've been good at hiding all my life. And, I've learned something new with my ability."

"What's that?" Devarius asked.

She grinned, closed her eyes, then channeled purple magic into her hands. Air flowed toward her, then it spread around her entire body, making it glow in a purple outline. Then, she disappeared.

Devarius stumbled backward, tripping over his own feet. Paedyn pointed at the empty space, his mouth opening and closing. Zaviana grinned.

Naveen reappeared.

Devarius got back to his feet. "You can turn invisible?"

She raised her eyebrows. "Apparently."

Chapter 29

Naveen shivered as she stalked out of Saefron's gate. She'd have been lying to herself if she claimed she wasn't nervous. No one was with her to help. She was alone. Chill bumps traveled across her arms. She began to lose her nerve. Her footsteps were cautious, slow, and not without shaking. She didn't know why she'd volunteered to do this, but it was too late now.

She did want an opportunity to practice her new ability, her invisibility. Naveen had figured it out quite by accident. The dragonscale was definitely the reason she could use magic, but when she'd discovered that her magic was different than Fraeyn's, she wanted to learn what else she could do that was special. Her dragonscale was purple, and after discovering it either came from a purple dragon or wyvern, and their abilities with wind and air, she began to play around. She'd been all alone when she maneuvered the air surrounding her hand to appear the same on both sides. It was like a mirror on each side of her with air, causing her appearance to completely disappear.

The ability took a lot of energy, at least as far as she'd learned it. Perhaps with practice it would get easier. However, she no longer had time to practice.

Whispers in the distance caused her to slow as she rounded a corner. None of the men were close to the wall, but their camp wasn't too far away. She noticed there was one large force at the main gate of Saefron, and a few parties separate from the main. She watched with interest as the few parties interacted with each other. All except for one. Naveen pinched her eyes closed as she focused on the group of men far away from the main camp on the western side. No one had interacted with them like the rest of the groups. If the empire were making men into shadows, Naveen believed they wouldn't be with the main army.

She tiptoed through the darkness, using the shadows of night to help hide her as she crept closer. Conversations began to become clearer.

"When are we going to attack? I hate waiting."

"I know. These resistance are scum."

"Who do they think they are? We all work hard and pay our taxes, and they think they can just come hide in the mountains without paying?"

"If they were paying taxes, I bet we'd get more from the emperor each paycheck."

Naveen's lips pressed tightly together as she slipped around the two talking men and toward a few of the others. She stopped when she saw a few shadows moving in the darkness. Air surrounded her, casting a light purple glow as her body faded into the darkness. She held the air around her as she continued to a tree.

More than four shadowmen stood fifty paces from her. They each had swords, and practiced against each other. Her eyes widened. The shadowman in the city had attacked during daylight. It was overcast, but at least the light of day made his shadow viewable. However, these four men, or shadows, could barely be seen in the darkness of night. They fought each other, clanging swords against one another. Their attacks were fast, faster than a normal man's should be.

Her eyes took in the rest of the scene. Besides the four shadowmen practicing, she noticed less than ten other men talking. One of them held a glass vial in his hand.

Naveen let the air surround her again as she crept closer. The air surrounding her kept her invisible in the darkness, but she still had to be careful with each step she took.

One of the men approached the man holding the vial. He grabbed the vial, moved it up to his face to look at it, then drank the whole thing in one gulp. Naveen froze, then carefully sat on the ground to watch. The vial of liquid was thick red, bubbles traveling up it constantly. The man who drank the liquid dropped to the ground, his body convulsing. Naveen wanted to go to him, to help him, but she dared not move.

The man's body transformed. It was no longer humanoid, but it pulsed from human to shadow for several long minutes until the transformation was complete. He lay on the ground for another few minutes before he rose to his feet.

Naveen turned around and began to crawl away. She noticed the other shadowmen, who were just practicing with swords a few minutes prior, began throwing magic at each other. Black fire flew from their fingertips. Some of it was aimed at the different shadowmen as they practiced, but some of it hit the grass around them, and it burned in a shadowy fire. It was the strangest thing Naveen had ever seen.

She made sure her cloak of air was secure around her as she crept closer to one of the fires. Naveen reached her hand out toward the fire and recoiled. It was hotter than a campfire.

One of the shadowmen collapsed onto the ground and began to spasm. His body flickered from shadow back to its natural form several times before the shadow completely went away. He lay on the ground, eyes closed. Naveen began to wonder if he was dead. A few of the humans dragged his body away to the man who offered the vials to them. He reached down, pressed his fingers against the man's neck, nodded, then continued to give another vial to someone else.

"Is he dead?" the man who received the vial asked.

The man shook his head.

Naveen crept closer to hear the conversation better.

"No, he's entered a coma."

"A coma?" The man looked sideways at the vial in his hand. "For how long?"

"Only a day this time."

"This time?"

The man grunted. "It depends how much of the dragon blood you drink. If you only do it once, you will gain powers for a full day, but then your body will crash, and you'll need a day to recover."

"It gets worse the second time you do it?" the quivering man asked.

"No, it gets progressively longer if you drink more dragon blood before your body crashes. If say, you drink the vial in your hand, and before the full day is over, you drink another vial, it will give you two days of power, but your body will crash for two days. Does that make sense?"

"Yes. I'm still not sure about this."

"You signed up to the shadowman project. Do you want the power?"

The man inhaled. "Yes."

"With power comes side effects. Be lucky it's as easy as this. Drink up, we have a lot of practice to do."

With one last look at the vial, the man drank its entire contents. His face twisted in disgust, then he dropped to the ground, convulsing.

One of the shadowmen stalked toward the man, his hands shaking. "I need more. I feel the effects wearing off. I need more. I must have more. Give me more."

The man smiled as he handed another vial to the addict.

Naveen turned around and began to run. She escaped the shadowmen's camp, but before she could reach the wall of Sae-fron, someone blocked her path. She crashed into him, then fell to the ground. His invisibility disappeared, and her strength was failing. Her energy was depleted and exhaustion began to overwhelm her.

A warrior in full chain mail looked down at her. His arms were crossed, and a large grin split across his cheeks.

"Well, hello there, what do we have here?"

He reached down, grabbing her by her hair.

Naveen screamed as she was dragged toward the camp.

Chapter 30

Zaviana paced the courtyard. Something felt wrong. She wasn't excited about the whole mission, but something was different now. Zaviana knew Naveen was more than capable, but still, to send someone out there alone to try and find a deadly secret .... She wished she'd gone rather than Naveen.

"Are you all right?" Devarius asked.

She shook her head. "No, I'm worried about Naveen."

Devarius nodded. "So I am. I don't think we should have let her go out alone."

"If we had more than one, we would have never gotten close enough to see or hear anything."

"I know ... but we have little choice now, don't we?"

Zaviana nodded.

"Perhaps we should give her a few more minutes ..."

Zaviana shook her head. "No. I'm leaving now. You don't have to come if you don't want to, but I'm going to search for her."

She turned away and stormed off. Only a few seconds passed, then Devarius was by her side. Ayla flew in the air above him, landed by his side, and walked next to him.

"Stay back, Ayla."

The wyvern tilted her head down.

"If I need you, I will call."

Devarius and Zaviana slipped outside the gate through a secret side entrance. Zaviana was impressed by how many ways into and out of the city there were. If she ever got the chance, she wanted to take a look at a map.

Zaviana noticed there were several camp fires around one larger camp. They were a ways off, but she stepped carefully to not arise suspicion. She scanned the area, searching for where Naveen would have gone.

"Do you see her?" Devarius whispered.

"No. And why are you asking me? My eyesight is the same as yours."

"There are several different camps. Which way should we go?" he asked.

Zaviana didn't answer. She brushed past him and around the stone gate. Naveen would have stayed close to the gate at first, and then if she saw anything, she would have tried to return the same way. Zaviana wasn't looking for Naveen, but for any traces of activity on the ground surrounding the gate. Nothing seemed out of the ordinary for a long time, but then she stopped. Her hand flung up, blocking Devarius from taking another step by her side.

"What is it?" he asked.

She pointed to the ground.

Snow made it easier to spot anything out of the ordinary. It also made it harder to hide. She saw Naveen's footprints heading toward one of the smaller camps, and she saw the footprints returning. She wondered how Naveen kept herself from being noticed for so long. Zaviana hadn't considered the footprints.

They'd have to check the way back inside to make sure it was covered up.

"What?" Devarius asked.

Zaviana knelt, looking closer at the ground. There was a dip in the snow. It was hard to see in the moonslight, but it looked like someone had fallen.

"Drag marks, look," Zaviana whispered.

Devarius' eyes grew wide. Something, or someone, was dragged from the spot in front of them, toward one of the smaller camps.

"Do you think that's—"

"Naveen? We need to find out."

Zaviana jogged into the night. Devarius looked around once before following close at her heels. The drag marks continued on for a long ways. It wasn't leading to the closest camp, but to another small one. Zaviana was glad it wasn't the main camp. There were too many dragons and warriors inside the main section.

Devarius bumped into Zaviana as she stopped to inspect the small camp.

"Sorry," he whispered.

Zaviana rolled her eyes as she hid behind a tree to watch the camp.

"Why do you think there are so many camps separate from the main one?" Devarius asked.

"There are many different specialties in the empire," Zaviana said. "And not all of them get along well with each other."

"What do you mean?" Devarius asked.

"Not everyone is a dragonrider. There aren't enough dragons. A few people are rather sore about that."

"So they'd rather not have the protection of the dragons at the main camp?"

Zaviana shook her head. "They'd rather do something to help the empire and stand out. Some of them do experiments, or research. If they can't ride a dragon, they want to impress the emperor in other ways. Being around the dragons distracts them from doing that."

Devarius nodded. "Makes sense."

"I found her."

"Where?"

Zaviana pointed to a makeshift cage in the back of camp. A woman sat on the ground with her back toward them.

"Are you sure that's her?"

Zaviana turned to glare at her brother. "Who else would they have as a prisoner?"

Devarius shrugged. "If Paedyn were with us, he'd have some kind of joke response. However, I'll just shut my mouth."

Zaviana smiled. "That sounds like a good response."

"So, how do we get to her? There's at least a hundred warriors in that small camp."

Zaviana closed her eyes. The wind around them picked up from a soft breeze to a raging storm. Snow began falling even harder, turning into a blizzard. Zaviana's eyes opened. They were white. Her pupils were gone.

"Are you doing that?" Devarius asked, his voice shaking with nervousness.

Zaviana smiled. She tried to look back at the camp, but the blizzard was too strong to see. "Let's go."

She rushed forward. Before she could make it a few steps, Devarius grabbed her hand. She paused, looking back at him.

"I can't see a foot in front of me. I don't know where I'm going. You have to lead me."

"Good," Zaviana said.

Zaviana held his hand tight as the two of them weaved through the storm. The wind blew hard, and the snow fell in large flakes, but Zaviana ran through the storm with little effort. She knew where each flake was, and where the wind blew. Her footsteps crunched into the ground, but their sound was flooded out by the raging wind.

They reached the camp easily. Zaviana bumped into a few of the guards on her way. They jerked in surprise, but before they could utter a word, Devarius unsheathed his blade and stabbed them through the heart.

"We're here," she whispered.

"Where?" Devarius asked.

The wind blew around them, creating an opening through the storm in front of Devarius. A cage with metal bars rested in front of them. Naveen sat, huddled into her legs with teeth clattering. Devarius stepped up to the bars and shook them. He searched the exterior, but couldn't find a way to open the gate.

"Devarius?" Naveen asked.

"Shh," Devarius whispered.

"One of the guards has the keys," Naveen whispered.

Devarius tried to pick the lock with one of his daggers. It was no use. He turned to search for his sister. She faced away from the prison, both of her hands in the air, surrounded by a white glow.

"Zaviana?" he whispered.

She turned to look at him, her hands still in front of her controlling the weather. Her eyes were still colorless. "What?"

"I can't open the cage. There's no key."

Zaviana clenched her teeth. Her energy was fading fast. She reached one of her hands behind her, separating it from stabilizing the weather. The storm above them flickered. Her right hand glowed in a blue hue as mist traveled from it to the bars of the cage. The storm raged harder, the wind grew worse, and the area around them became harder to see as her control of the storm faltered. Ice crept up the metal and wood bars, and Naveen stepped away from them.

"Now!" Zaviana yelled.

"What?" Devarius asked.

"Strike the bars!"

She fought to hold her hands steady, separating her power between the storm and the prison bars.

Devarius didn't have to be told twice. He stepped forward, unsheathed his sword, and slammed it against the frozen bars. The bars shattered.

Naveen ran out of the broken prison as Zaviana's hand dropped to her side. She ran into Devarius, wrapping her arms around him. He hugged her briefly, then pushed her aside.

"We have to go," he said.

"Now!" Zaviana said.

Her body trembled; her other hand dropped. She fell backward. Devarius rushed forward to catch her in his arms.

"Are you all right?" he asked.

"I can't ..."

"What?"

"I'm drained. I can't walk."

Devarius clenched his teeth. "I'll carry you."

"The storm won't last," she whispered.

"Then I better hurry." He lifted her over his shoulder. "Come on, Naveen. Follow me, hurry!"

He ran out of the camp with Zaviana in his arms and Naveen at his heels as the storm around him disappeared into a light snowfall.

A battle horn echoed in the camp behind him.

Chapter 31

Devarius leaned back in his chair, his hands running over his short hair. He looked at everyone sitting around the table. These were the leaders of the resistance. Without each and every one of them, they would fail. Everyone had their own ideas, but this is where all their ideas could come together. They needed a plan.

Naveen sat next to him, shivering a little bit. They'd just returned to Saefron and she was still a bit shaken up. Devarius had demanded an immediate council meeting. Now he looked at the faces of the others: Zaviana, Ellisar, Tynaer, Paedyn, Lilianya, and Orrick. Each person had something special to add to the plan.

"Well, why have you called us all here?" Tynaer said.

"As some of you know, we were attacked this afternoon in the city. The attacker was hard to see. It was as if he were a shadow."

"A shadow?" Lilianya asked.

"Yes. You could see his shadow, but not him, or rather, the shadow looked like it was a man, but it was a bit distorted, like looking into a river and when you put your hand in the water, it's disjointed."

"The bending of light," Ellisar said.

"Yes." Devarius nodded. "This was something like that. Well, we decided to investigate. We sent Naveen outside the gate to try and learn something."

"Alone?" Lilianya said.

"Yes," Devarius admitted. "After a time, when she hadn't come back, Zaviana and I grew worried, and we went to find her."

"What did you find?" Ellisar asked Naveen.

Silence filled the room as everyone stared at Naveen. A cold sweat ran along her forehead. She was still cold from being in the blizzard, and a blanket was wrapped around her.

"They have shadowmen. I saw at least five of them. If they were hard to see during the daylight, they were nearly impossible to see at night."

"What are these shadowmen?" Tynaer asked.

Naveen gulped. "As you either saw or heard today, these men can literally transform into a shadow. It is frightening. What is even more frightening is how they do this. From what I've seen and heard, they have hundreds of vials of dragon blood. It's thick, bubbling, and red. They keep it in vials, and the men drink it. When they do, their body disappears, replaced with a shadow."

Ellisar's eyebrows rose. "Dragon blood?"

Naveen nodded. "That's what they called it. I don't know if they mixed anything with it, but they called it dragon blood."

Ellisar shook his head. "Leave it to Galedar to torture the dragons another way to give him more power."

"There is a drawback," Naveen said.

"What?" Tynaer asked.

"The effects only last for a full day. After that, the man passes out from exhaustion. His body sleeps for an entire day before he regains consciousness."

Paedyn raised his brows. "So, all we have to do is survive for a day. No problem. We attack when it's nap time!"

Naveen shook her head. "However, if they have another vial to drink as they're getting weak, before they pass out, it will last another full day."

Ellisar raised an eyebrow. "How does that affect their exhaustion?"

"They will be in a coma for two days to recover," Naveen responded.

"I wonder how long they can do this, or, how far some of these men are willing to take their bodies for recognition from the emperor," Ellisar said.

"Is there anything else?" Devarius asked.

Naveen shook her head. "They can use magic. I saw them cast a black fire at each other for practice."

Devarius gulped. "Please tell me that's all."

She nodded.

"Then it is time to talk about plans. What can we do to stop them? We need ideas on how to stop these shadowmen and the dragonriders. There are also thousands of warriors outside who don't have sick magic or dragons. If they break our defenses at the gate and enter our city, what can we do to defend?"

"What about wyvern blood?" Tynaer asked.

"What?" Devarius asked.

"If dragon blood can give such powers, can wyvern blood do the same? I know they're not as powerful as dragons, but even if we can make shadowmen last half as long, perhaps we could—"

"No," Devarius interrupted.

"Devar—"

"No. We will not be collecting blood from the wyverns. It is inhumane. They are our allies, not our livestock."

"Perhaps we should ask them—"

"I said no."

"Devarius," Ellisar interjected.

Devarius faced the leader of the resistance. "There are other ways."

"What ways?" Ellisar asked. "What other choices do we have?"

"Dragonscales. We've collected a bunch of dragonscales. We just need to figure out how to use them, like Naveen has."

"And how has that worked out for you? Have you found anyone besides Naveen and Fraeyn who can use the scales?"

"No," Devarius admitted.

They'd carved and cleaned hundreds of dragonscales off the carcass of a dragon, but no one they gave them to had been able to use them. At first they wondered if it was the dragon-scales themselves, but when given to Fraeyn or Naveen, they could use them to create fire. It was everyone else who couldn't use them. Perhaps there was no real magic in the scales.

"We are talking about a matter of life and death here. Whatever we decide, whether it's humane or not, is going to impact all of us in Saefron. If we choose to do nothing, and all die, then was it worth it?" Ellisar asked.

"What you're suggesting—"

"Is a chance to defeat the empire here and now. After we defeat them, we can decide what is moral and not. But if we lose, then we will never have that chance. I have collected dragon blood myself, with Alora's blessing. I had a feeling it could be used for something, but I didn't know what at the time."

"You're no better than the emperor if that's what you believe," Devarius spat.

He stood, took a last look with cold eyes at Ellisar, then stormed out of the room.

Devarius wandered the streets, unsure of where to go. He was heated, and frustrated. How could Ellisar call himself noble, fighting for a good cause. What would happen if they defeated the empire and Ellisar were to take the emperor's place? He claimed to not want power, but peace throughout the land; however, Devarius began to question his actions. Siphoning dragon blood? How could that ever be right?

He walked into the abandoned forge. Crates and crates of vials filled with wyvern oil filled the room. Why did they need blood? They had tons of wyvern oil. Surely they could find a way to better use it. Devarius paused as he looked at all the crates. Was he just as bad as the emperor and Ellisar? He was siphoning wyvern oil from the creatures. It was with their consent, but Ellisar claimed he had dragon blood with his dragon's consent. Yet, Devarius had stormed out of the room, furious with him anyway.

Footsteps edged close from behind him. Devarius turned around, his hand on the hilt of his sword. Ellisar stood in the room. No one else was with him.

"I'm sorry," Devarius said.

"I understand your anger, Devarius. I am not happy with this situation either. I don't want to use these kinds of tactics. But, you have to remember, the emperor will be, and a lot worse. He will do whatever it takes to wipe us out. He won't even care if he loses his entire army to do it. Because, without us, there is no hope for the rest of Kaeldroga."

Devarius bent his knees to nearly sit on the ground. His hands were on top of his head, rubbing it furiously. He didn't know what to do. They weren't ready to face the Dragonia Empire yet.

Ellisar walked past him to a desk. A wooden vial holder sat on the desk, and a vial of each color of wyvern oil was displayed inside, cork caps protecting the contents. He ran his finger across the outside of each vial. Blue, green, gold, and red.

"I wonder if these have the same effect as dragon blood," Ellisar whispered.

"What?" Devarius asked.

"This wyvern juice you've been milking."

"I'm not milking it," Devarius snapped.

Ellisar raised his eyebrows.

"All right, I'm sort of milking it."

"Do you think it gives abilities like the dragon blood if ingested?"

"I've touched it. The fire juice burns, so does the ice—frostbite. I can't imagine it being safe inside of you."

"But have you drank it?" Ellisar asked.

"No, and no one else should."

Ellisar grabbed the blue vial to inspect it closely. He bit his bottom lip and tilted his head.

"No, Ellisar," Devarius said.

"Why not? It's worth a try."

"It would be suicidal."

"You don't know that," Ellisar said.

"I will have no more deaths at my hand," Devarius said through clenched teeth.

"It wouldn't be your choice to make."

Devarius snarled as he stood. He took one last look at Ellisar, who was still inspecting the vial with wonder in his eyes. Devarius stormed past him and out of the room. He would be no part of this. Too many innocent lives had been lost, and Devarius wouldn't be a part of anything that may harm any more people. He needed air, and a hard drink.

Chapter 32

Vibrations shook through Devarius' bedroom, knocking him onto the floor. His eyes sprang open. Thunder pounded outside. He got to his feet and slid on his leather armor. Once he secured his scabbard, he rushed out the door.

Flames covered the ground. Bells rang throughout the city. People ran through the streets, many of them clueless about what to do.

They were under attack. Devarius glanced to the sky. Dragons and wyverns flew around each other in circles. They blew elements at each other, but many of them missed. Every now and then, a dragon would lower its neck to look at the ground, and flames would erupt toward the city.

"Ayla," Devarius called.

Paedyn stepped out of his room across the street. He was still in his nightclothes as he rushed to the center of the road to peer upward. One of the dragons blew fire.

"Paedyn!" Devarius yelled.

Paedyn dove forward, rolling toward Devarius. The flames missed him by inches. Devarius helped him to his feet.

"Are you all right?" Devarius asked.

"Why do they get to make fire?" Paedyn said. "I want to make fire. Pyro! Where are you, you no good coward wyvern!"

A growl echoed along the street. Paedyn turned around to see Pyro inches from him. He grinned at the wyvern. "Oh, there are you. Are you ready for flames?"

Paedyn climbed onto Pyro, and the two of them flew into the sky. Devarius rolled his eyes. His friend was foolish, he'd always known that, but to fly into the sky without even donning armor was pure lunacy.

Ayla dropped to the ground in front of Devarius. The groom had her saddled and ready to ride.

Hello, little one.

"Are you ready?" Devarius asked.

Quite.

Devarius climbed onto Ayla's saddle and secured himself before patting her side. She ran forward five long steps, then leapt into the air. They soared into the sky to join the fight.

Devarius looked down, and shivers traveled along his spine. He'd been flying Ayla for a long while now, but he never got used to being so high up. Devarius had hoped the battle wouldn't start so soon—it'd only been three days since bringing Naveen back. He'd known it was coming though. The anticipation had been killing him. Now it was over, all the long waiting was finished. The war had begun.

Arrows soared into the sky. Ayla dipped to her left, then right to dodge them. Devarius held on tight. He wondered how much the arrows were helping, and how much they were a hindrance. The arrows crashed into the underbelly of a dragon and bounced off. Ayla had to shift again to avoid them.

"Come on," Devarius said through clenched teeth. "Use the oil!"

Ayla arched upward, and all the blood rushed to Devarius' head. He held on tight as his head began to spin. Ayla twirled in circles to her left, making him even more dizzy. Fire blazed all around them. Finally, Ayla evened out, then blazed ice from her mouth. The blue mist hit one of the dragon's wings. Its mobility suffered as it tried to balance itself with one usable wing. Ayla flew closer. She reached her claws out to grab the frozen wing. Her claws tore into the wing, and her teeth bit a large piece of flesh from the dragon.

The dragon snarled, turned its head around, and snapped at Ayla. She tried to escape, but the dragon's talons wrapped around her leg. Devarius unsheathed his sword. The dragon's mouth leaned in, its jaws wide, heading toward Ayla's throat. Devarius waited. When the dragon's head was close enough, he jumped up, thrusting his sword into the dragon's open mouth. The sword penetrated its flesh and pierced through its snout right between the eyes. It released its grip on Ayla. Devarius dropped back into his saddle, groaning as the impact to his groin hurt him. Ayla dove, then spiraled to the side to escape the falling dragon. She flew higher, and the two of them watched as the dragon dropped to the ground.

Thanks.

Devarius smiled. "Who's next?"

They scanned the battle below them. The empire was coming in strong. At a quick glance, Devarius counted more than a hundred dragonriders. He wondered how many dragonriders the empire had.

Wood rattled in the distance, and Devarius turned to glance the other direction. The army outside the gate of Saefron was loosing arrows into the city, and they gathered around the gate.

"Ayla, fly to the gate!"

Ayla didn't ask questions. She obeyed. Once they were close enough, she ceased flapping her wings and glided in the wind current.

More than a hundred strong men held a thick tree trunk in their hands, and they continued to bash it into the gate. They reared back, then ran forward, over and over again. The echoing wood rattled.

"We need to do something, Ayla. I don't know how much longer the gate will hold!"

Oil?

Devarius patted his chest pocket. "Yes." He scratched his chin. "Which vial should I use?"

Depends. How well can you aim?

Devarius grinned. "Well enough."

Green.

"Green?" he asked.

Acid burns through wood.

"Right. We'll need a distraction. They have two dragonriders guarding the gate. Any suggestions?"

Paedyn.

Devarius laughed. "Can you reach him?"

Ayla closed her eyes and went silent for nearly a minute. Her eyes opened and she nodded.

"Did you reach him?"

Before she could answer, a massive wyvern dove from o
head to levitate in front of them.

"I am told a distraction is needed. Do not fret, do not fear,
Paedyn is here."

Devarius chuckled.

"What's the plan, boss?"

"Boss?"

"You do have a plan, don't you? I mean, what kind of person doesn't have a plan?"

"You," Devarius said.

Paedyn shrugged. "Well, I don't count."

"We need to protect the gate. I need you to distract those
two dragonriders protecting them. Ayla and I will sneak in as
you're distracting them to destroy all the tree trunks they have
prepared to bash our gate in."

"One question," Paedyn said.

"Yes?"

"Can I use fire?"

"I would expect nothing less from you," Devarius said.

"One more question."

"What?" Devarius sighed.

"If this works, can I get a toy boat?"

Devarius rolled his eyes.

"What? You told me I could get a toy boat ages ago."

"I will make you a toy boat myself!" Devarius said.

Paedyn frowned. "It better be a good one."

Devarius shook his head.

Paedyn grinned, then he and his wyvern flew off into the
distance.

Devarius watched as Paedyn flew away. True to his style, Paedyn wasted no time in angling his wyvern down to begin blazing fire on the edges of the gate entrance. They slipped through the two dragons and blew another blast of fire, making flames burn on each side of the men with the tree trunk. Several of the men grew scared and ran away. More took their place. Some of the men who ran were struck down by their own captain, which caused the rest of them to press on. They slammed against the gate again.

Paedyn and Pyro flew high up into the sky, blazing fire all the while. The two dragons chased after him. Pyro made rings of fire in the air, then flew through them, doing loops and spins all the while. They looked like a circus act.

Ayla dove toward the men attempting to breach the gate. She opened her mouth and sent a blaze of icy mist over all the men, causing all of them to turn a light blue with frostbite. Ayla flew past them, then circled back around.

Devarius held his vial ready, and as she slowed, he dropped it. Two seconds went by before it shattered on top of the half-frozen tree trunk. True to Ayla's word, the acid began eating the tree, dissolving it into nothingness. Ayla circled back around, hovering over the two other tree trunks ready to be used. Devarius dropped a red vial on them. It shattered, then burned the battering rams.

We need to go, Ayla said.

Devarius glanced up and noticed the two dragons flying down toward them. They'd given up on chasing Paedyn in endless circles. Though Paedyn turned toward them and Pyro tried to burn their riders from the backside, they didn't take the bait.

The dragons maneuvered away from the flames and continued toward Devarius.

"Go!" he shouted.

Ayla flew upward toward the two dragons. The two massive flying beasts were close together, flying toward them.

"Fly between them!" Devarius said.

She didn't question him, but continued forward. The dragons opened their mouths, ready for fire. Devarius shivered, praying he wouldn't become dinner.

"Ice!"

Her mouth opened and a light blue mist burst forth. Devarius fixed a blue vial to his slingshot and launched it forward. When it met her ice breath, the vial shattered at the same time as the flames came. The ice turned to water and followed the fire into the dragons' mouths.

Ayla slipped between the two creatures. Devarius grabbed the dagger on his left leg. He threw it toward the rider on his left. The dagger struck true, penetrating the rider's neck. Then he unsheathed his sword, held it steady with two hands, and slashed it into the rider on his right. His aim struck true, and the dragonrider's head flew into the air.

They continued up into the sky for several long seconds before Ayla turned around to watch as the two dragons crashed into the camp, slamming into hundreds of warriors. People screamed at the camp.

Devarius smiled. "Great job, Ayla. Let's get back into the city to help the others."

Chapter 33

Pyro dipped low as fire blazed in the sky above them. Paedyn laughed as they spun in circles, dodging dragon after dragon. Pyro circled around the two dragons to their backside.

"Fly close to them from behind, then blast their riders with fire!" Paedyn shouted.

Pyro dipped her head down and glided toward the back of the left dragonrider. Paedyn snatched a vial from his sash, a large smile on his face as he prepared to throw it at the dragonrider to his right.

Flames erupted from Pyro's mouth. The dragonrider screamed as the fire consumed him.

Paedyn tossed the vial toward the other dragonrider. It missed him and shattered at his side. The rider turned around to look at them. Paedyn waved at him.

You missed.

"Nope, I didn't."

Pyro had begun flying away, but now curious, she turned her body around and flapped her wings forward, causing her to fly backward.

Paedyn stretched his head to the side so he could watch as the dragon tried to make a sharp turn to face them. Before the

dragon fully turned, the saddle came loose, burnt f·υ...
Paedyn had thrown on it. Before the dragon could approach
them, the saddle completely came off the beast, and it, along
with the rider, rushed toward the ground. The dragon dipped
down, trying to catch its rider.

"Stop him, Pyro!"

Pyro nose-dived after the dragon. Fire blew from her
mouth to nip at the dragon's tail. The dragon turned its neck
around to blow flames toward them. Pyro shifted, dodging the
attacks. Paedyn held on tight as Pyro had to shift from left
to right to dodge attacks. They continued to fly toward the
ground. As it grew closer, Paedyn frantically hit Pyro's side.

After one last blast of fire from the dragon, Pyro pulled
up to even out. The dragon wasn't so lucky. It crashed into the
ground on top of its rider. The whole earth quaked at the impact. Paedyn as glad he was in the air so he couldn't feel the
near earthquake.

"That was fantastic, Pyro. Let's do it again!"

A shadow overcame them. Paedyn looked around, spotting
a large dragon blocking the red sun. He patted Pyro's side to direct her toward it. She complied, flying toward the dragon.

Paedyn's mouth dropped as they approached the beast. It
was easily twice as large as any other dragon. Instead of red like
the others, it was a reddish black, and fiercer than anything Paedyn had ever seen.

"Wow, that's a big dragon," Paedyn gasped.

Pyro snorted.

"Don't worry, I like you better."

Pyro shook her head from side to side.

"Take us closer."

Closer? she asked.

"Yes, closer. We can't let that dragon get the surprise on everyone."

Paedyn ... I can't defeat that.

"Of course you can't. But we can. Or, at least, we can try."

They approached the dragon from behind. Paedyn's hands trembled as they neared. It was larger than he'd thought. The rider on the creature's back wore black robes and a hood. Paedyn exhaled a deep breath. He clutched at the last acid vial in his hand. They would need to make this count. If this dragon descended on Saefron, they were all in danger.

When Pyro flew close enough to attack, the dragonrider turned to look at them. Paedyn froze as he stared at the rider. Shadow cast over the rider's face, making Paedyn see nothing but darkness. Who was this rider? Whoever they were, they were powerful and important.

"Now!" Paedyn screamed.

Pyro's flames soared through the air. The dragon moved. Pyro's flames missed. Paedyn's jaw dropped. The dragon was massive, but it moved faster than any other dragon.

"Who is this?"

Paedyn ... I don't have a good feeling about this.

"Get us closer. I need to use this vial on them. It's our only hope."

Pyro did vertical circles in the air to dodge flames from the massive beast. She evened out when above the dragon. Flames erupted from her mouth. The dragonrider held out his hands, and as the flames reached him, they separated to each side of him. Not a single flame touched the rider.

"Hold your flames steady to keep him distracted," Paedyn called.

Pyro continued to blaze her flames.

"A little bit closer," Paedyn said.

Pyro continued flying toward the creature. Paedyn clutched the vial in his hand. He judged the distance, then with all of his might, he threw the vial. It spun around in circles in the air as it approached. The rider saw it and released his hold on the flames, causing them to burn his clothing. His hands moved, his right touching his chest as his left arm stretched out. A blast of purple energy flew toward the vial from the rider's hands. It enveloped the vial, halting it in midair.

Paedyn's jaw dropped. Pyro ran out of air, her fire ceasing. The vial hovered for several long seconds. Then the dragonrider shifted his hands, bringing his left hand to his chest and flinging his right arm forward. The vial of acid began to fly toward Paedyn and Pyro. His eyes widened.

"Fly, Pyro! Retreat!"

Pyro spun to the side, then dove toward the ground. Paedyn glanced up and saw the vial arching down to follow them.

"Faster, Pyro!"

Pyro continued on, shifting from left to right as she descended. No matter which way she went, the vial followed. Paedyn grew dizzy as she descended, but he kept his focus on the vial above them. He reached to his side and pulled his rapier from its scabbard. Paedyn loved the weapon. He'd helped craft it. But he knew it would be worthless to him if he were dead. He locked his legs in the saddle, holding his rapier with two hands, and glanced up to find the vial only feet above them and traveling fast. Paedyn steadied his weapon, aimed, then let go.

The rapier only took a second to impact with the vial. It shattered. The rapier disintegrated.

Acid filled the air. Pyro ran out of steam. The acid splashed over Pyro's side as well as Paedyn, though it wasn't as bad as it could have been. Most of the acid separated, and sprayed in a large arch all over Saefron, which was better than a concentrated explosion on top of them; at least, for them it was better. Paedyn only hoped he hadn't condemned too many people inside Saefron to death.

Pyro lost control. Her wing was burned badly from the acid. They spiraled toward the ground. She tried to spread her wings to slow their fall, which helped, but they still hit hard. Paedyn reached his hand out to graze Pyro's neck as he lost consciousness and blackness overtook him.

Chapter 34

Zaviana stepped back as she watched Paedyn and his wyvern crash into the ground. Silence filled the city for several long moments as a cloud of dust filled the air. Archers ceased their attacks, warriors lowered their shields. Zaviana shivered as she approached the scene. Everyone fled the area before the impact. Before she made it more than a few steps, she sensed the acid in the atmosphere. She froze, her eyes glowing purple, then she cast a magical barrier to block the acid from reaching the city and all the innocent lives around her. Zaviana reached out for more energy and funneled the air to her shield. After a long pause, she used the air to push her shield outward, dispersing the acid back into the air.

Paedyn was still on the wyvern's saddle, but he did not move. The wyvern, however, tried to get to her feet. Zaviana rushed over to the beast. She laid her hand on the creature's snout, trying to soothe her.

Paedyn, Pyro transmitted into Zaviana's head.

Zaviana moved her hand away from the wyvern's snout. She untied Paedyn from the saddle, and with help from those around her, brought him to the ground. Her fingers found his pulse in his neck and she let go of a long-held breath.

"He's alive," she whispered.

Good, the wyvern said.

"He will need medical attention. Can you two take him to the medic bay?" Zaviana asked two of the archers next to her.

They two men nodded, then grabbed Paedyn's head and feet. Zaviana watched as they disappeared toward the city's hospital.

When she turned around to face the wyvern, she noticed her trying to get to her feet. The wyvern's movements were erratic. Half of the creature's body was burned from the acid, including parts of a leathery wing. She would not be able to fly until healed.

"Easy now, girl," Zaviana said.

I have to get up. I have to help.

Zaviana shook her head. "No. You are too hurt. You need to rest. You need to heal."

I can't. They need me.

"No. Paedyn needs you. He will need you by his side when he wakes up."

I can't abandon them.

"You aren't. You need to rest before you can help your kin. But, right now, you can be of help to Paedyn. Will you stay with him? Will you comfort him?"

The wyvern cringed as she glanced back to see her damaged wing. I can, she finally said.

Zaviana and a few of the others around her helped the wyvern to her feet. With aid, the wyvern was led to the infirmary to be by Paedyn's side. Zaviana helped all the way to the door, before turning around to glance up at the sky. She felt so useless on the ground. The battle was happening in the sky.

There was little she could do. She was worried if she tried casting magic into the sky, the target would move the opposite direction, and instead of being useful, she'd only make matters worse.

A shriek up above startled her. Zaviana glanced up to see another wyvern falling to the ground. The battle above was devastating, and Zaviana had a hard time following it. Another shriek came from the wyvern. Zaviana looked closer. The wyvern wasn't hurt. It landed on the ground, sniffing something that had impacted only moments before.

Zaviana approached the purple wyvern. When she got closer, she noticed the dead human on the ground. Resistance colors were on the fallen man. It was her rider. The wyvern sniffed one last time, then tilted its head back to shriek into the air. Zaviana stepped closer. The wyvern looked at her, head tilted, eyes watering.

"It's all right, girl."

No, my rider is dead.

"I know. There's nothing I can do about that. But don't let your grief overtake you. There is still much that can be done."

The dragons need to die. They are cruel beasts. At first, I thought they were intelligent like us. Foolish was I. I tried to communicate, to ask them why they attacked.

"Did they respond?" Zaviana asked.

No. They didn't say a word.

"We need to stop them."

Yes.

"We can't let your rider's death be in vain."

It won't be.

"We can stop them."

I." Zaviana reached her hand up toward the wyvern.

The purple wyvern sniffed Zaviana's hand. I don't need another rider. I can fight them myself.

"Please," Zaviana said. "I want to help. There is little I can do down here."

What difference could you possibly make up there?

Zaviana grinned. She held her hand out, palm up, and a small ball of fire formed. "Enough."

The wyvern tilted her head. She reached her nose down to sniff the ball of flame. When it burned her, she recoiled.

All right, little one. I will allow it.

"What is your name?" Zaviana asked.

Yasmirah.

"Nice to meet you, Yasmirah. I'm Zaviana. And with your help, we're going to make the difference." Zaviana climbed onto the wvyern's saddle.

I hope so.

Yasmirah leapt into the air, and together they searched the skies. An epic battle was taking place all around them. The wyverns outnumbered the dragons, but not by much. Zaviana hoped it would be enough, but she knew if she didn't discover a way she could help, their chances weren't likely. Yasmirah dodged several bursts of flames. Zaviana held on tight, growing a bit dizzy. She wondered if sky sickness was a thing—after all, she did get seasick.

A dragon to the west fought against two wyvernriders, and was winning. Zaviana directed her reins to tilt Yasmirah toward the battle. When they approached, the dragon was nearly at the rear of one of the wyverns. Its mouth opened wide, not with flame, but with intent to bite, and with its massive jaw, it would destroy the wyvern.

Zaviana opened her mouth to speak, but before she could, Yasmirah's mouth opened, and a beam of wind shot to the dragon. It caught the dragon inside the mouth, spinning its head around with whiplash. Zaviana grinned. She couldn't have done a better job herself. The wyvern followed the dragon, using her wind ability several more times to knock the dragon off balance.

Zaviana decided it was her turn. She closed her eyes and felt the energy all around her. Moisture filled the air, though cold and frozen in the form of snow, it was still there. She could redirect heat to melt the falling ice, turning it to water, but she wanted something more. Positive and negative charges filled the air. Each cloud held electrical current, and Zaviana could feel the molecules in each one. They would only need to be shifted slightly to become deadly. A grin formed on her face. She moved the electrical current around inside of two clouds on each side of them.

Lightning flashed from one cloud to the other. It missed the dragon and its rider by a hairbreadth. The next flash though, they weren't so lucky. The rider was zapped off of his saddle, screaming all the while as he fell to the earth. The dragon tilted down, ready to try and save the human, when thunder followed. Zaviana reached to cover her ears. It was loud, and shook the atmosphere near her. The sound startled the dragon, and while it was distracted, Zaviana shifted the electrical elements once more. Two bolts of lightning, this time one from each cloud, flashed toward the lone dragon. The current remained for a long while as they fed into the dragon. Zaviana held her ears tight as the thunder rolled. She could have sworn she saw the creature's bones through the lightning, but she couldn't be sure.

The lightning faded, and the dragon dropped to the earth. It was either dead or unconscious, but after the fall from hundreds of feet in the air, it wouldn't matter either way. A shadow formed overhead, blocking out the winter clouds. Zaviana glanced up and saw a massive dragon above them. It was larger than any other she'd seen.

"Yasmirah, take us around to the side of that dragon so we can see it."

The wyvern didn't respond, but did as she was told. She circled around twice, then cut to the side and gained altitude. When Zaviana saw the dragon and its rider, her jaw dropped.

"No," she whispered.

What? Yasmirah asked.

"This isn't good. This isn't good at all."

What is it?

"The emperor."

Who?

"The one who is leader over all the Dragonia Empire. He never leaves his chambers, let alone his castle."

Then we must defeat him. If he is no more, perhaps victory will be ours.

Zaviana shook her head. "He's too powerful."

We have to try. I saw your magic, your lightning. If we cannot defeat him, who can?

"No one," Zaviana whispered.

We have to try.

Zaviana gulped. "You're right. Prepare yourself. This will not be an easy foe."

Prepared.

Yasmirah climbed higher and flew closer to the emperor. Zaviana shivered. She closed her eyes, becoming one with the elements around her. All she had to do was defeat him, no sweat, no problem. She shivered again. Big problem. A deep breath calmed her, but she still wasn't ready. How could she defeat the emperor? There was little she could do against his torture in Dragonia, what could she possibly do now? Yes, her abilities had grown, but not that much.

It felt like only yesterday that the emperor was torturing her with his fire. Zaviana had spent years as his prisoner, and he'd done everything in his power to try and break her. He'd come close several times. His magic, his fire, was hard to tolerate. A cold sweat covered her face as they approached the massive dragon. She wouldn't let fear overcome her. Zaviana was stronger than the fear. She was stronger than the emperor made her out to be; she had to be, or she would fail.

"Are you coming back to me, child?" the emperor called.

Zaviana clenched her teeth. He was so close. She watched as he let down his hood, showing his old, wrinkly skin, yellow eyes, and black, pointed beard.

"Your reign ends here," she spat.

"Is that so?" He scratched his chin. "And I suppose you're the one to stop me?" He laughed. "Honestly, I thought they would do better."

He was toying with her. Yet, it was working. Anger consumed her.

"I am enough," she muttered through gritted teeth.

"Are you?" he spat.

Flames erupted from his dragon, arching toward her in a spiral. Yasmirah dodged the attack, then blew wind toward the dragon. The creature shifted slightly, but otherwise the wind had no effect on the massive dragon.

Zaviana closed her eyes. She concentrated on the cloud once more. Lightning zapped out of the sky, reaching the emperor. She felt the energy being rearranged before she knew what was going on. When she opened her eyes, the lightning was heading straight for her and Yasmirah.

"Fly, Yasmirah!"

Yasmirah turned sharply to their left, avoiding the lightning. She flew hard away from the dragon, but the lightning continued to follow them. Zaviana stared in disbelief behind them as the bolt of lightning trailed them by mere feet. She closed her eyes and concentrated. The lightning was too powerful to stop, but she could divert it. She focused her energy to a nearby cloud, mixing up its elements until it became a negative charge. The lightning was inches from touching Yasmirah's tail when it flashed the other direction.

Thunder rolled, creating large vibrations in the atmosphere behind them. Yasmirah trembled back and forth as she tried to ride the air waves to safety. Zaviana held tight.

Once the thunder settled, Zaviana focused again. She gathered the cold and the moisture surrounding her and directed it toward the emperor, who stayed on their trail.

It looked like the sheet of ice would strike them, but instead, it moved to the side as the emperor redirected it. He tossed it aside like it was nothing. He was too powerful. She didn't know how she was going to stop him.

"Keep flying, Yasmirah! Keep flying!"

I don't think we can fight him.

"I warned you."

There is no time for blame. We must escape.

"No, you're right. We need to stop him. We may not survive, but even if we only inflict a little bit of damage, it may help."

How?

"He has one flaw."

What flaw?

Zaviana grinned. "He's arrogant."

How are we going to use that to our advantage?

"Trust me. Turn around. We fight."

Yasmirah hesitated for only an instant before complying. Zaviana saw the surprise on the emperor's face when they looked back at him.

"Wind," Zaviana whispered.

When Yasmirah opened her mouth, Zaviana shifted a sheet of water and a sheet of cold in front of her mouth. Her powerful wind first traveled through water, which froze, before it blasted toward the emperor.

The emperor raised both of his hands as he blocked the attack, shifting the elements in the air to redirect the ice storm back toward them.

"Fall," Zaviana whispered.

Zaviana reached to create a shield. The ice storm crashed into them. Yasmirah ceased flapping her wings, and the two of them fell out of the sky. Zaviana's shield faltered. She'd had a suspicion it might. The emperor was much more powerful than she was. Ice impacted Yasmirah's wing, and she shrieked.

As they fell toward the ground, Zaviana saw the grin on the emperor's face. His arrogance showed. Zaviana released the rest of the energy that she'd been holding. Two massive icicles lingered in the sky above the emperor and his dragon. They struck the dragon's wing and the emperor's back at the same time. The dragon wailed as it tried to control itself in the sky. It slumped sideways, floating crooked in the sky as an icicle over a meter in length penetrated its wing. The ice shard penetrating the emperor's back was a lot smaller, but just as effective. He fell sideways, gripping his reins tightly as he tried to keep from falling.

Zaviana had failed to defeat him, but she'd succeeded in injuring both the emperor and his dragon.

"Are you all right?" Zaviana asked.

Hurt. Hurt bad.

"Hold tight. Try to land easy. I will use my ability with the wind to help."

Yasmirah continued to fall unsteadily. Her left wing was injured, but her right was strong. However, that wasn't enough to keep her steady. Her right wing flapped against the wind to slow their descent, but the left barely moved. It looked like one of the cartilage on the wing's exterior had snapped out of place. With only one wing working properly, Yasmirah spun around in circles, trying to use her one wing to steady them. Zaviana grew dizzy fast. She had to close her eyes to be able to concentrate. Once she could see all the molecules around them with her eyes closed, but her mind open, she was able to push air in the opposite direction against Yasmirah's left side. It steadied them enough to see as they crashed to the ground.

Yasmirah's feet hit hard, but not as hard as they would have without Zaviana's help. The wyvern's legs fell from under her, and they tumbled forward onto the ground.

Zaviana untied herself from the saddle and rolled out of the way as Yasmirah attempted to get to her feet.

Pain.

"Yasmirah?"

Hurt.

"Yasmirah?!"

The wyvern groaned.

"We're about to have company."

Yasmirah struggled to her feet. She was weak, unsteady, and injured.

Zaviana glanced around. They were outside of Saefron.

"We're on the wrong side of the wall," Zaviana whispered.

They were at the southern entrance. The entire Dragonia Empire camped nearby as they tried to breach the gate. They had seen them crash to the ground. More than a hundred warriors ran toward them. It would be several minutes before they arrived, but Yasmirah was in no condition to fly.

Yasmirah growled. Zaviana unsheathed her sword. They awaited their fate, but they weren't going to give up without a fight.

Chapter 35

Naveen stepped back, her jaw dropping as she witnessed the destruction of the gate. Warriors flooded inside. The resistance put up a stand at the entrance, but it wasn't enough. A dragon was what made the final push to shatter the stone gate. Men shrieked as the dragon stepped inside and began eating them. Naveen watched in horror.

She unsheathed her sword and waited as they broke through. Naveen refused to give up without a fight. But how much could she really do? She was still a novice with a blade.

Her fist opponent approached her. His blade slashed at a downward arc toward her left shoulder. She curved her blade upward, slamming the sword aside. He followed up with three swift mid-strikes toward her abdomen. She blocked two of them with down-handed swings before stepping backward to miss the third. Growling, he rushed toward her, two strikes to her right side, one to her left, then an uppercut toward her belly. She parried each strike with ease. Naveen could feel the wind surrounding her. The purple scale on her necklace glowed. She wondered if she were actually using magic, or if it somehow had protected her. Naveen could remember her defensive blocks, yet, she still stood. She pushed her blade down, forcing the man's uppercut to fall toward the ground. He was left defenseless. She stepped forward, slid her blade backward, then swung hard over her right shoulder to his neck. It hit hard. His head didn't fall off like she'd thought it would, but he fell nonetheless.

Naveen glanced back to the gate. Shadowmen entered the city. She saw almost a hundred of them. Her eyes widened and her mouth dropped. They couldn't fight against so many shadowmen. Naveen could barely see them. The sun had set, and shadows blended into the darkness.

She backed away. Fear overcame her. She couldn't fight this. No one could fight this. She backed away into an alley. A shadowman saw her and approached.

Naveen barely raised her sword in time to block a blow. She didn't know how she saw it, but she held a defense against a shadow blade. He struck again, and her sword moved on reflex to her right, again intercepting the strike. She felt the air around her, and trusted it to guide her. Every molecule around her body pulsed with energy as she struggled to defend herself against the shadowman. His blade came again, and her sword moved to intercept the strike. She felt her arms being pulled more than her doing the blocking. Her eyes tried to focus, but a shadowman inside of a dark alley was impossible to see. Three more strikes came, and she blocked each in turn, one of them she felt she blocked herself without the aid of magic. Gaining a little confidence, she pressed an attack on the shadow. Left, right, left, left, uppercut. The shadowman grunted at her last strike. She'd struck him. Before she could appreciate her small victory, he came at her fast. His slashes were so fast that even with her magic aiding her, it wasn't enough. After the tenth straight strike, her sword flew from her grasp to clatter onto the ground. A deep gash poured blood from her forearm. She clutched it with her opposite hand as she backed away. The shadowman approached. His face was blacker than any shadow she'd ever seen. His eyes were black as well, and the grin that split his face in two was also black. He enjoyed his victory, and he'd enjoy his kill. His sword rose in the air. Naveen closed her eyes as she dropped to the ground on her bottom.

After several seconds when nothing happened, she heard gurgling. Naveen shivered as she opened her eyes. A sword pierced the shadowman's heart. Black blood stained the blade. The man crumpled forward, falling off the sword.

Cederic stood behind the shadow, her sword in hand. His face showed no emotion. He stabbed the sword into the ground and held out his hand. She grabbed his hand cautiously, and he helped her to her feet.

"Are you all right?" he asked.

Naveen shook her head.

He grabbed her arm to inspect her wound. Naveen flinched, her teeth clenching with the pain. Cederic cut a strip from the front of his cloak with a dagger, then wrapped it around Naveen's arm. He tied it securely as he grabbed her sword out of the ground.

"Come on, we need to get out of here," he whispered.

"Where?"

He shrugged. "Inside."

She tried walking forward, but she stumbled. Her head was fuzzy.

"Can you make it?" he asked.

"I—"

Cederic stepped up to her, grabbed her, then lifted her over his right shoulder. He held her sword with his left hand as he carried her out of the alley.

Everything around Naveen looked blurry, and she had a hard time concentrating. Cederic was careful as he rushed onto the main road, then opened a door and slipped inside. He gently set Naveen on the ground. She leaned against the wall as she took in the room they had entered.

Hundreds of bubbling vials of different colors filled open crates in the room. The leader of the resistance, Ellisar, stood in the center of the room. He held a bubbling blue vial in his hand, twirling it between his fingers. After a deep breath, he turned to look at them.

"Ellisar, the city is being overrun!" Naveen screamed.

"I know," he whispered.

"Are you going to do something?" Naveen demanded.

He turned to face her. "What? What would you like me to do? I am one man. There are thousands of them."

"Our warriors are out there, fighting and dying—for you! For your purpose, for your skewed idea of freedom. We can't be free if we're dead."

Ellisar closed his eyes. "I hoped for so many years that this would turn out differently. But, it seems, they found us before we could build enough of a defense."

"There has to be something we can do." Naveen wept.

"I only have one idea, and I don't know if it will work."

"What is that?" Cederic finally spoke.

Ellisar held out the vial. "Naveen saw men drinking vials of dragon blood to turn into shadowmen. What would happen if one of us drank this wyvern oil?"

Naveen's eyes widened.

"Would we turn into our own variation of shadowmen?" Ellisar continued. "Or would it kill us from the inside out?"

Silence filled the room. No one spoke. Everyone stared at the vial of blue oil in Ellisar's hand.

"I'll try it," Cederic said.

Ellisar and Naveen turned to him.

"What?" Naveen asked.

"I'll try it," Cederic repeated.

"No," Naveen said, her voice shaky.

Cederic spun to look at her. "What would you have us do? Hide in this room until all our warriors are dead? After that, they'll come for us. We need to do something. We have to try it."

"But ... it could kill you."

Cederic knelt in front of her. He touched her face, gently rubbing his thumb against her cheek. "If I do nothing, we all may be dead anyway."

He stood, turned, and strode toward Ellisar. He snatched the vial from the leader's hand, popped off the cork, and drank the entire vial in one gulp. Cederic looked back to Naveen. Tears fell along Naveen's cheeks as she stared back at him. He smiled at her, then his body went rigid. The vial dropped from his grasp, shattering on the ground. His body trembled, convulsing furiously as he dropped to the ground. He was having a seizure. A blue haze covered his skin. Fog filled the room, coming from Cederic's body. The room grew cold as frost formed around Cederic's body. His eyes closed.

"Cederic!" Naveen screamed.

She tried to get to her feet, but Ellisar rushed to her. He held her back. She sobbed as she clutched at his leg.

Something scraped against the ground. Naveen wiped her tears and looked up. Cederic sat up. His face was no longer pale white, but it was as blue as the sky, and even his hair was blue. He smiled at her as he pressed his hands on the ground at his sides and rose to his feet. His steps were slow and steady, and he took one last glance at Naveen, then shuffled toward the door. He raised his hands in front of him. Blue ice escaped his fingertips, slamming into the door and blasting it from its hinges. He grinned, grabbed Naveen's blade leaning against the wall, and stepped outside.

Chapter 36

Zaviana's hands glowed purple as she held the energy surrounding her at bay. Time was running out. Several hundred men from the empire's army rushed toward them. As they neared her range, she let go of the energy. A silver light blazed through the air to zap into the first man. Electricity traveled through his body and into the next. The magic traveled through fifteen of the warriors, and they lay on the ground, clutching their stomachs in pain as they vomited. Two of them died shortly after.

The attack paused the next line of men for only a moment before they gained courage and continued toward her. Zaviana wondered how long her strength would last before she'd be depleted. She held her breath and began to focus on the elements surrounding her again.

Rest, little one, Yasmirah said.

Zaviana turned to look at her new friend. The wyvern stood tall, stretching its legs, its damaged wing hanging limply by its side. Her massive jaw opened, and Zaviana clutched the rock by her side. Wind more powerful than any storm rushed from the wyvern's mouth. It collided with the first hundred men, throwing them all up into the air nearly a hundred feet and throwing them back into the main army. The men screamed all the while as they fell to their deaths, many of them injuring or killing others in the crowd.

"Well done, Yasmirah," Zaviana whispered.

Zaviana hoped it would deter the rest from approaching, but all it did was grant them more bloodthirst. Hundreds more men took their place as they charged toward Zaviana and Yasmirah.

Unsheathing her sword, Zaviana sighed. The first men approached, and she swung her sword to the left, then right, using the dancing butterfly sword form. She spun around time and time again, stabbing her sword through one victim's stomach to the next. Her skill outmatched theirs, but she also felt the magic surrounding her, guiding her movements. An extra sense took over her moves, her mind, showing her where the next attack would be. She moved, guided by the power to block, strike, and kill. Another three down, two slashed across the throat and the third stabbed through the heart. Her senses tingled with danger to her side. She reached her left hand in the air, and it glowed blue as ice trickled from it to freeze three men in solid ice to her left.

Yasmirah roared into the sky, then blew again, tossing another hundred men into the air to crash hundreds of feet away.

Zaviana was growing weak as she battled, and she knew Yasmirah was as well. Maces fell toward her face, and she slipped to the ground. Her sword arched up in time to deflect the two weapons. She jerked her elbows backward, then slashed at their knees. The two men collapsed onto the ground. Zaviana didn't have time to end the two injured men as two more took their place with swords swinging low. She deflected both strikes, then stabbed one in the gut while blasting the other away with power guided by her left hand. Yasmirah blew into the wind again, tossing another dozen men away. They didn't fly hundreds of feet anymore, but only half the distance. They were growing weak, too weak.

"We won't last much longer," Zaviana whispered.

Then we give it our all. We die with as many of them as we can.

Zaviana nodded.

Another hundred men rushed forward, weapons held high. Zaviana screamed into the air. She used her weapon to steady herself. Fatigue overtook her. Her muscles ached; her hands shook. She spread her feet further apart to keep her knees from collapsing.

A roar tore through the sound of battle. It came from above; it came from behind. The charging men halted, skidding their heels against the dirt. All of them looked up into the sky, eyes wide, jaws dropped, weapons falling to the ground or held high in defiance.

Zaviana turned around and looked up. A giant blue dragon flapped its wings in the sky behind her. The dragon's mouth was spread wide as it roared again. As it neared, blue mist sprayed from its mouth onto the unsuspecting warriors. They didn't cry out or scream as they instantly became entrapped in solid blue ice.

Zaviana's eyes grew wide as the dragon passed them. It circled around again, exhaling another breath of ice from its mouth. In a matter of seconds, everyone who'd charged Zaviana was frozen in ice. The dragon and its rider turned their attention to Zaviana as they approached.

Who is that?

"Derkas," Zaviana whispered.

Who? I thought only Ellisar befriended a blue dragon.

"There was one other."

The dragon landed in front of them. Her body tilted to the side to allow the dragonrider to climb down a ladder that rolled out. Derkas climbed down, a wide grin across his face.

Zaviana's cheeks heated, turning an even darker brown. Shivers created bumps across her arms as she took a step back. Her breath caught as she watched him approach.

What is that gooey warm feeling you're expressing?

Zaviana flinched. "Get out of my head," she whispered.

"Zaviana."

"Derkas."

"Did you think you escaped me?" he asked.

"Escaped? If I escaped, then was I truly a free woman?"

He grinned. "You're always free, Zaviana. I just wanted to protect you."

"You can't protect me from everything, Derkas."

"Clearly." He laughed.

"Thank you," she said.

He raised an eyebrow. "What for?"

"Saving me ... yet again."

"I ought to be good for something."

"I thought you were going to stay out of this conflict," she said.

Derkas shrugged. "You needed me. You know how much I hate to disappoint."

Zaviana's eyes shifted from left to right. "Too many people saw you. They will know you attacked the empire. He will know."

Derkas' shoulders arched. "Nothing can stop that now. The most important thing is that you are safe."

Zaviana's skin tingled as his hand touched her cheek. She closed her eyes as she welcomed his touch. He was warm, inviting, and everything she needed at that moment.

"It's good to see you again, Zaviana."

She opened her eyes and smiled. "You too."

"I take it you won't run away with me?"

Zaviana shook her head.

Derkas sighed. "Well, what can I do to help you?"

"They know you are the one who gave them up to the empire," she admitted.

He nodded. "You told them, I suppose."

She pressed her lips tight and closed her eyes. After a deep inhalation of breath, she said, "I had to. I had to warn them. They had to be given the chance to defend themselves."

Derkas raised his eyebrows. "Lot of good it did them."

"They're stronger than you give them credit for, and I'm not abandoning them."

"Very well. How can I help you?"

Zaviana glanced to the city. The gate was broken, and hundreds of men from the Dragonia Empire flooded into the city.

"My wyvern is injured. Help me take her into the city through the gate. Then help me seal it."

His eyes widened. "Seal the gate?"

"Yes."

"How do you want me to do that?" he asked.

Her eyes twinkled. "An ice wall."

His chin touched his chest as he glared at her with eyes wide. "Even if Chalce could make an ice wall, it won't hold. Their dragons have fire. Fire melts ice."

"We don't have to stop them. We just need to slow them down. Trust me."

Derkas took a deep breath. He held his hand out, palm up, toward the gate. "After you."

Zaviana smiled. "Come, Yasmirah."

They ran toward the gate. Derkas mounted his dragon and flew into the sky. Zaviana looked back to see him one last time as she continued on. The gate was flooded with hundreds of soldiers as they marched into the city. Derkas flew over them. His dragon breathed ice over the direct line of soldiers, freezing them all solid. With another pass, a large span of men was frozen in ice outside the gate. Men yelled with frustration. Chalce landed in front of the gate, shattering several of the ice statues into pieces. Her tail slammed around to crush dozens more. The men behind the frozen statues ceased moving as they watched with horror. Chalce continued to pulverize the frozen men into dust with her tail and paws.

Zaviana and Yasmirah reached them through dozens of frozen men. She tried her best not to look at the ground at the hundreds of shattered ice particles that had once been humans. Her foot crossed the threshold of the city, then she was jerked backward. An arm wrapped around her bicep. Derkas looked into her eyes.

"I will go no further," he said.

Her mouth parted, and her eyes widened slightly.

"They will not welcome me in there. You know that. If I enter the city with you, I will be seen as an enemy. I will have to fight the empire and the resistance."

"I can speak to them, I can—"

Derkas' finger pressed against her lips. He shook his head. "No. This is where we part."

Zaviana fought back tears. "Will we see each other again?"

"I hope we do. I will seal this entrance, and I will do what I can out here to disrupt their attack, but I dare not go inside."

"Derkas ... I—"

He kissed her. His lips were warm against hers. A spark traveled from him to her, sending shivers down her spine. His hand reached to her face, where it swept her hair behind her ear. She melted into him, clutching at his shirt with her long fingernails.

He pulled away. "Now, go."

She opened her mouth to argue.

Derkas shook his head. "You're needed. Go."

Zaviana wiped her eyes before rushing into the city. She tried not to look back, but she did one last time. Derkas wasn't clear anymore. She saw him through thick blue ice as it grew in place of the shattered gate. Zaviana gulped, unsheathed her sword, and ran into the city.

Chapter 37

Devarius stood in Saefron, horrified by the scene playing out before him. He'd joined the resistance to stop the tyrannical rule of the empire. He'd found the wyverns, siphoned their oil, and given the resistance hope. Now, as he looked around, he wondered what hope was left. They were overrun. The battle in the sky was failing, and the battle on the ground was nearly lost. He wanted to do something, but there was little he could do.

He charged forward, his sword held high. Ayla was at his side, using her ice breath to freeze one after another. The warriors weren't too difficult to defeat. Devarius had been trained well by Orrick, but the shadowmen disturbed him. The resistance hadn't completely fallen yet. They had warriors, hundreds of them, and they were battling against the empire, but Devarius knew they wouldn't last.

"What hope is there?" he said to no one.

We need to reach the gate. It's our best chance to stop more from coming in.

Devarius wanted to argue, wanted to tell Ayla it was hopeless, but he bit his tongue. He nodded. They had to try.

His sword flashed in the air, striking through the gut of another solider. He'd lost count of how many he'd killed. Devarius wished he didn't have to kill men. He wished he could talk to them, tell them how foolish they were for blindly following the emperor, but he knew his words would fall on deaf ears. He fought on, striking down one opponent after the next, staining his sword crimson.

The gate came into view. Not many soldiers blocked his path. Most of them had already spread throughout the city, and he could only hope the resistance's warriors could handle them.

A wyvern stepped through the gate, followed by a woman. Devarius' fists clenched. There was help. He needed to reach them, to help them. Devarius refocused his attack, pushing forward with renewed passion. If they could make a stand at the gate, if they could prevent more of the empire from entering the city .... He dared not hope.

"Ayla, make a path for the gate. We seek an ally."

Ayla leapt in front of him, swinging her tail to slam several warriors into the air to crash into the sides of buildings. Devarius rushed to her side, deflecting a blow aimed for her throat. He swung his sword three times, knocking the man's weapon to the ground. Devarius slammed his sword into the defenseless man's throat. It didn't go through his entire neck, but the man dropped to the ground, lifeless.

Devarius pressed forward. He became one with the blade. Catching Butterflies, Stalking the Grasshopper, Swatting the Bee. Each form he transitioned to flawlessly. Compared to the easy victims in front of him, he was a blade master. He'd never thought his skill impressive, but he realized why Orrick had trained him so hard, and why he'd used such ridiculous tactics to get him to learn. He was better for it.

After the way was clear, Devarius looked around one last time. Seeing no one, he rushed forward to meet his ally. He skidded to a stop as he watched with disbelief as the open hole where the shattered gate had stood began to fill with solid ice. He watched with mouth agape and eyes wide.

Devarius' eyebrow twitched. "Zavi?"

The woman turned to face him. "Brother." She smiled.

"What are you doing here?"

"Blocking the entrance to Saefron. You?"

His eyes bulged even further. "You did this?" He pointed to the ice wall blocking the entrance.

Zaviana shook her head. "No, I don't believe even I am that powerful. My wyvern and I crashed outside of the city, and we had to fight our way back in. We had help getting back into the city, and help sealing the entrance."

Devarius raised a brow. "Help from who?"

"It isn't important."

Devarius twitched his lip from left to right. "It kind of is."

She shook her head. "I'll tell you another time."

"And since when do you have a wyvern?"

She smiled. "Her rider fell, and I helped her. We've bonded."

He rolled his eyes. "At least it's not Paedyn's wyvern. Come on, we have to help take back the city. There are hundreds more empire soldiers in here."

Zaviana nodded as she unsheathed her sword. The two of them rushed toward the center of the city. They saw skirmishes happening everywhere, and paused as they looked from left to right.

"Where do we start?" Zaviana asked.

Devarius scanned the courtyard where most of the skirmishes were taking place. He paused as he noticed something. His hand sprang forward, finger outstretched.

"There."

"What?" Zaviana asked.

"Shadowmen. We need to focus on the shadowmen. If we can defeat them, the rest of our warriors will have a better chance of overcoming the others."

Zaviana nodded.

Devarius dashed across the courtyard. He unsheathed his sword, bringing it up in the nick of time to deflect a shadowman's blade. Devarius snarled, shoving his sword forward with a push from his shoulder. Metal clung as their blades hit, but other than the sound of metal, it was hard to see what was going on. Only a small bit of torchlight lit the shadowman's features. Zaviana rushed to Devarius' side, stabbing her blade through the shadow's heart. They nodded to each other as they turned away to face more of the shadowmen.

"There are too many of them," Zaviana whispered.

More than twenty shadowmen surrounded them, making a circle. Devarius gulped as he searched the area for anything they could use to their advantage. A blue light caught his attention. He tilted his head as he tried to see what it was. A lone man rushed toward them, his entire body aglow in blue light. Streaks of blue left his fingertips as he fought against empire soldiers and the shadowmen. Anyone who was in his way was frozen in solid blue ice. Ayla began to help him, and together they froze several more shadowmen and a dozen warriors.

"Who are you?" Devarius asked.

The man smiled as he approached. His skin wasn't white or brown, but instead, a light blue to match his fiery eyes.

"What are you?" Devarius asked.

Devarius furrowed his brow as he looked at the man. "Shoemaker? I mean, Cederic."

The man grinned. "Yes.

Devarius' eyes widened. "You drank the oil?"

Cederic nodded.

Devarius closed his eyes and inhaled. When he opened them, he noticed dozens more men approaching. Each glowed—purple, red, blue, yellow, or green. Elements came from their fingertips as they attacked the invading army.

Devarius swallowed his fear. He wanted the oil to be useful, but he didn't want this. Devarius wasn't sure what the effects would be, and he didn't want anyone hurt because of the oil he'd collected. It was too late now. All he could do was hope for the best. As he scanned his surroundings, he noticed something he hadn't dreamed of. The tides were turning. They were defeating the empire inside of Saefron. The resistance was starting to win.

Devarius grinned. "Thank you for your help."

Cederic nodded, stepped past Devarius, and pointed his hands to the sky. Blue ice flew from his fingertips to strike a dragon's wing. The beast roared, then crashed outside of the city.

Devarius watched with fascination for a moment, then looked at Zaviana. "Come on, there is still much work to do.

We need to make sure we've defeated all the empire inside of Saefron."

Zaviana nodded, and the two of them ran away from the courtyard full of glowing icemen, firemen, lightning men, wind men, and acid men. Devarius paused one last time to look at all the elements filling the sky and inside the city from the new warriors. He shook his head in disbelief. Magic. The secret to magic was the wyvern oil all along.

A loud roar silenced the action in the city. Devarius looked up to see a dragon larger than any he'd seen before. The dragon landed in the center of the courtyard, breathing fire in a large area in front of it. People ran screaming. The fire struck resistance men and empire men alike. Shadowmen shrieked and fell, but so did the elemental men of the resistance. They all burned and crumbled to the ground.

"Oh no," Zaviana whispered.

Devarius turned to face her. "What?"

"It's the emperor."

Devarius' eyes nearly popped out of his sockets. He closed his eyes as he heard the dragon roar into the sky once more. Devarius looked around the city.

"What are you doing?" Zaviana asked.

"We have to stop him."

"We can't fight someone that powerful. I tried. He defeated me in the sky. That's why my wyvern and I crashed outside the city."

Devarius bit his top lip as he looked at her. He ran over to a mounted ballista. Zaviana followed him.

"What are you doing?" she asked.

"Whatever it takes to stop him," Devarius snarled.

He unfastened thin rope from one of the torches by his side. Reaching into his sash, he withdrew several vials of wyvern oil. He left their corks on as he held them to the tip of the ballista bolt to tie them to it with the rope.

"Those won't stay on. The bolt releases too fast."

"I know." Devarius raised his eyebrows.

He grabbed the large glass jar next to the ballista. Blue wyvern oil bubbled inside of it. He poured the liquid over the glass vials at the tip of the bolt. Ice formed at the tip, locking the vials to the bolt.

Zaviana's lips scrunched together in a circle as she watched him. Once the ice formed completely, he dripped some of the oil on the tip of the bolt, then threw the jar in the air toward the dragon. It shattered on the ground, and the snow transformed to ice.

"Distract them," Devarius whispered.

He stepped behind the ballista and angled it down toward the dragon.

Zaviana's eyebrows scrunched together as she looked back to the emperor. She took a deep breath, then collected as much energy as she could. As she exhaled, her power rushed forward. Yellow lightning flashed from her fingertips toward the emperor. He saw the attack and blocked the magic; however, he didn't see the bolt as it approached at the same time. It struck the shoulder of the dragon and exploded, knocking the emperor off the beast. The dragon flew across the city to crash into the side of a building.

Devarius grinned as he unsheathed his sword. Zaviana staggered next to him, drained of energy.

"Where do you think you're going?" she asked.

"To stop the emperor."

He clenched his fists as he charged toward the fallen emperor. Devarius grinned as he neared the man, but his grin faded when the emperor stood. His hands reached up, and an orange glow trickled from his fingertips. Devarius raised his sword to block the incoming fire. He didn't think it would work, but the element bent around the sword as he charged. When Devarius was close, the emperor had to relinquish his power. Devarius raised his sword high, prepared to strike.

When his sword came down, it met with a blade. The emperor snarled. Devarius grinned. He couldn't face magic, but a sword—that he could do. Their weapons spun in various patterns back and forth, but neither could gain traction on the other. Devarius considered himself skilled in sword fighting. He was trained by Orrick. There were a select few who could match him with a blade, and all of them had been trained by Orrick. However, the emperor was strong. His parries flickered at unbelievable speeds, and his attacks were even fiercer. Devarius had a hard time blocking them. He even had to back away as he clutched to his sword as tight as he could to prevent it from flying from his grasp.

Their battle went back and forth for what seemed like forever. No attack Devarius could deliver did anything to unbalance the emperor. Left, right, left, left, middle, uppercut. Nothing worked. Devarius tried all of the sword forms Orrick had trained him in, even intermixing a few, but nothing worked. The emperor was a master.

Devarius pressed on. He wouldn't give up. If he could destroy this man, if he could defeat him, they could win the war against the empire. There was no one else in power to continue it. It would be a long battle of politics and battles before any re-al progress was made, but they would be leaderless. He shifted his pose, inviting the emperor to go on the offensive. The man smiled, but accepted his offer. Devarius could barely block the flurry of strikes that came at him. He wasn't a better swords-man than the emperor, but he had been learning, studying the emperor's attacks, his arrogance.

The emperor's sword stabbed straight. Devarius knocked it aside. It swung left, right, left, right. Each attack was narrowly blocked by Devarius. Another stab went straight at Devarius. His block slipped, and the emperor's blade slid to slam through Devarius' side. The emperor grinned. Devarius grinned back, raising his eyebrows. The emperor frowned, his mouth open-ing, then his eyes went rigid as Devarius' sword slammed into the emperor's armpit.

Devarius' blade fell to the ground, as did he, backward onto the ground. Pain raged in his side, but it was worth it. He'd hurt the emperor as well. Devarius hoped it was enough. He was out of energy, and without a sword.

The emperor approached, his sword held steady in his right hand as his left arm hung limply at his side. Devarius crawled backward, blood staining the ground as he moved. Before the emperor could reach him, someone appeared out of the shad-ows.

Ellisar.

"Galedar, it's been a long time," Ellisar said.

Galedar grinned. "Ellisar. I suspected you were the face of this so-called resistance."

"Your lust for power is your weakness," Ellisar said.

"And your belief that without power people can be controlled is yours."

"That is the difference between you and me. I never wanted to control people. I want people to be free."

Galedar shook his head. "You saw the war that happened when people were free. Free people are foolish. They kill each other. The empire is the only way to keep them reined in."

Ellisar dipped his head. "That is where we see differently, my old friend."

Galedar raised his sword. "Let this be over, friend."

Chapter 38

Ellisar and Galedar crossed swords. Each man was a sword master. Their blades moved so fast it was hard for anyone else to see what was going on, or who had the advantage. At first, it seemed the emperor was winning, but the fight turned around just as fast. Neither man was able to inflict a wound on the other.

Devarius backed away, searching for some way he could help. Zaviana appeared at his side, reaching her hand down to help him up. He accepted her help gratefully.

"We need to do something to help," Devarius said.

Zaviana shook her head. "There is nothing we can do. This is their fight."

"We can't do nothing," Devarius pleaded.

"We can help the rest of the city. Not all of the empire warriors have been defeated yet."

Devarius nodded. He knew she was right. There was little they could do to help Ellisar's fight. Devarius had already tried to battle Galedar once, and he had been outmatched. He could only hope the injury he'd inflicted on the emperor would help Galedar defeat him.

Devarius and Zaviana joined the fight in the city. There weren't many empire soldiers left, and they were able to make short work of chasing them down. They didn't have many elemental warriors left after Galedar's dragon had destroyed most of them, but it was enough to fight off the force of soldiers inside the city.

Devarius grew tired as he slashed his blade from one solider to the next. He'd been training relentlessly for months for endurance, but it wasn't enough; he was growing tired.

Zaviana was exhausted as well. She used her magic a few times, but most of her aid came from her sword. Devarius was impressed with his sister's skill with a blade, and he wondered where she had learned it.

Once the rest of the threat had been eradicated, Devarius and Zaviana found themselves back at the courtyard. Everyone was at the courtyard, watching with fascination as Galedar and Ellisar fought.

Neither man seemed to tire, and their blades still moved at the same fast speed as before.

Galedar pressed hard against his old friend, his sword making a flurry of strikes from the left to the right. The technique he used looked like a mix between Dancing Fireflies and Swat the Bees. His blade moved seamlessly in circular arcs from the left to the right. Each swing was deflected by Galedar, but it appeared as if Ellisar was gaining. His stance changed halfway through a swing to angle toward the emperor. The strike hit true. Galedar cried out in pain as Ellisar's blade struck the same shoulder Devarius had injured earlier.

Devarius swung his fist in the air with a grin.

Galedar slowed for only an instant. Then he pressed back hard against Ellisar. His attacks came fiercer, less controlled, but more powerful. Ellisar backed up as he tried to deflect the emperor's offbeat offensive strikes. He succeeded in blocking most of them, but then his ankle twisted, causing his stand to falter. Galedar didn't hesitate as he slammed his sword down hard. Ellisar blocked the blow, but staggered as he did. Galedar pressed forward, slamming again and again, until finally, an opening appeared in Ellisar's defenses. His blade pierced Ellisar's gut. Ellisar didn't cry out in pain, but he did fall. Galedar stood over him, his sword held out, and a grin plastered his face.

Devarius snarled as he unsheathed his sword and rushed toward the emperor. His sword blocked the strike meant to kill Ellisar. Galedar smiled.

"Have you come back for me to finish you off?" Galedar asked.

"I believe you have that wrong," Devarius whispered.

He thrust his blade forward, but Galedar blocked the strike. Devarius pushed forward. He noticed the emperor was tiring, not as much as a normal man, but he was slower than before. Devarius had had a break, the emperor hadn't. His sword flashed as he used Dancing Firefly. He moved his body to the attack, his legs hiking high with each strike. Devarius used his whole body for each strike, leaning forward, pushing his leg and knee forward with his strike. It was working. Devarius was on the complete offensive. Galedar barely kept up with his defensive blocks, but he was keeping up.

Clumsy footsteps pounded against the earth to the side of their battle. Devarius' eyes shifted as he saw Galedar's dragon approaching. The beast was injured, and limping the whole way, but it was still more powerful than Devarius. When the dragon neared, its mouth opened. Flames erupted from the creature toward Devarius. Devarius flinched, but he dared not take his attention away from Galedar. If he did, he would certainly die.

Before the flames could reach him, a blast of ice breath intercepted them. The air from the fire blast continued forward, and a warm rain began falling sideways against Devarius and Galedar. Devarius didn't need to turn around to know Ayla was there. She was protecting him.

Thank you, Devarius said in his mind.

You're welcome, little one. You need to finish this. I can't stop this dragon forever.

I'm trying.

Devarius pressed on. He noticed the emperor's blocks growing less precise. Devarius' eyebrows furrowed. He pressed on, changing forms to Swat the Bee. It was a more sporadic attack, more random. He was gaining an edge. His sword broke through Galedar's defenses. He slashed the emperor's weapon down, then shoved the sword into Galedar's gut. Galedar stepped away swiftly, but the damage had been done. He immediately refocused and was able to block the rest of Devarius' attacks.

The dragon roared, a roar louder than any he'd heard. His dragon was mad. Galedar brought his hand in front of his body and used magic to push Devarius back. Then Galedar ran to his dragon.

"Attack!" Devarius yelled, pointing his sword toward the emperor.

Arrows flew. Dozens of them bounced off the side of the dragon as Galedar climbed the ladder up the beast's side.

"Use the oil!" Devarius shouted.

More arrows flew. Many of them were doused in ice wyvern oil. Parts of the dragon began to turn blue and tried to freeze. The dragon growled as it frantically spat fire on itself to warm its body.

Devarius ran forward as the dragon was distracted. He approached the beast, slamming his sword into the dragon's chest. It penetrated through the scales, but not by much. The dragon shrieked as it looked down. It tried to blow fire, but nothing came from its throat but wind. The breath was enough to blow Devarius off his feet. His sword fell with him, falling out of the dragon's chest. Blood stained its tip, a deeper crimson than anything else he'd seen.

The dragon leapt into the air. Its wings flapped as it attempted to exit the city. Before it could flee too far, a ballista bolt pierced its wing. The dragon faltered for a moment as it used its good wing to help propel it from the city. Its flight wasn't pretty, but it had enough strength to exit the city.

Devarius turned around to see Naveen at the mounted ballista. He smiled at her. They hadn't defeated the emperor, but they had won the battle. The tide had turned.

Chapter 39

Devarius rushed into the city, Zaviana at his side. He went through alleyways until he found the shop he was looking for. Stepping inside, he gasped. Half the vials he'd brought with him were missing. His teeth clenched.

"What are you doing?" Zaviana asked from behind him.

"We need to finish this battle," Devarius said through clenched teeth.

He opened his sash and carefully began placing vials of wyvern oil inside.

"What do you plan to do?" Zaviana asked.

"Ayla and I will take to skies to join the rest of the wyvern-riders."

"My wyvern is injured. I can't join you."

Devarius smiled. "It's all right, sister. I can handle this."

"I want to help."

Devarius wrinkled his nose. "How hurt is your wyvern?"

"Her wing is damaged."

"Is it broken?" he asked.

"I don't believe so. I think it's dislocated."

Devarius grabbed an extra blue and red vial. "Let me try something."

Zaviana bit her lip. She gathered several vials to put in her sash. Then she followed Devarius out the door.

"Call her," Devarius said.

"Yasmirah," Zaviana said.

The purple wyvern approached them. Devarius put both vials in his left hand as he reached out with his right. Yasmirah sniffed him, but stood rigid.

"It is all right, Yasmirah. Trust him."

Yasmirah leaned down, showing Devarius her injured wing. Devarius reached his hand up and touched the injury. Yasmirah whimpered. He cupped his hand around the joint attaching the wing to the wyvern's body and squeezed gently. The wyvern snarled.

"It's not broken. I believe you're right, Zavi. It looks to be dislocated. I believe I can pop it back into the socket, but it will hurt ... a lot."

"Yasmirah?" Zaviana paused as she listened. She turned to Devarius and nodded. "She will allow you to try."

"Tell her not to eat me." Devarius grinned.

Zaviana laughed. The wyvern snickered.

Devarius grabbed the joint again, this time with both hands, and shoved it back into place. The wyvern shrieked and flung its wings back.

"Calm down, girl. Here, this will help."

Yasmirah relaxed a little, but her wings shivered. Devarius removed the cork to the fire oil. He poured a small amount on the joint. The wyvern moaned as the oil caught aflame, burning lightly on the wyvern's joint. Devarius capped the vial, then grabbed the ice oil. He slowly poured it over the soft flames at the wyvern's joint. The flames disappeared, and ice took its place, forming over the joint with frost radiating from it.

Devarius capped the vial, then placed it in his sash with the others. "It's not a perfect fix, but the heat and cold should help soothe the ache. You'll still need to rest for a few days, but at least for now you should be able to fly. That is, if you want to."

Zaviana smiled. "Yasmirah?"

Devarius raised his brows.

"Let's go," Zaviana said.

Devarius called Ayla to him. He climbed onto the saddle, and they flew into the sky. Zaviana and her wyvern were right behind them. Devarius grinned. It was time to end this battle.

The dragons were outnumbered, with the wyverns gaining an edge. Galedar and his dragon were nowhere to be seen. Devarius flew up to circle one of the dragons giving several of his wyvernriders a hard time. Ayla flew over the dragon, and Devarius dropped one of his ice vials. It shattered onto the wing of the dragon. Ice entrapped the wing, causing the dragon to falter and begin to glide toward the ground. Devarius left the dragon, letting his wyvernriders finish off the beast as he focused on the next.

Zaviana wasn't too far away, fighting her own foes. Devarius watched her use magic as well as the vials she'd taken to defeat several dragonriders. He was proud of her.

Devarius refocused on his own opponents. He and Ayla circled around dragon after dragon, throwing vials and blasting ice, and Devarius used his sword to slash at the wings of the massive dragons. From spins to loops, they fought. The dragons were overwhelmed by the hundreds of wyvernriders.

Together, they fought against the remaining dragonriders until the odds were so much in the favor of the resistance that the rest of the dragons fled. Devarius grinned as he heard the signal for retreat. Ayla and he watched as the dragons fled. They continued to attack, but not as vigorously. Devarius wanted them to keep retreating and not try to take one more wyvern out as they fled. He signaled for the rest of the wyvernriders to join him as they pushed the dragons out of the city. Devarius was done with the battle. He wanted it to be over, but for it to truly be over, they had to achieve victory. If the dragonriders only retreated to outside the city to regroup before another attack, it wouldn't be good enough.

Outside the city, the empire was regrouping. Devarius snarled. He raised his sword in the air, and wyvern roars surrounded him as his wyvernriders pushed past him to attack the camps. Fire, ice, acid, wind, and lightning blazed the camps of the Dragonia Empire. Men fled their camps, grabbing what supplies they dared, and traveled west. The dragonriders attempted to fight back, but they were overwhelmed with the power of the wyvernriders. They dared not relent, and with the dragons grouped together, it was easier for the wyverns to use their elemental powers to strike multiple dragonriders at a time.

A battle began between the remaining dragonriders and the wyvernriders. All the men on foot were fleeing the mountain, but the dragonriders remained. Devarius entered the battle, fighting his hardest. He saw less than a hundred dragonriders remaining, and they still had at least two hundred wyvernriders. Many of his allies and friends had fallen, but not all. There were many of them injured back in Saefron.

Devarius pressed on, his sword swinging hard against the wings of dragons. Ayla's breath froze as many wings as she could, and Devarius depleted the rest of his vials against the remaining dragonriders. They defeated three more of the dragonriders before they fled with the rest of their army.

The wyvernriders began to cheer their victory. They didn't chase the army or the dragonriders, but a few wyverns continued to spit their elements at them with satisfaction. The battle was over. The empire had lost. They'd saved Saefron ... for now.

"We did it." Devarius grinned.

Yes we did, little one, Ayla said.

Chapter 40

Ayla landed in Saefron with Devarius on her back. The rest of the wyverns followed. Everyone dismounted as they cheered. Men and woman came out into the streets. They began cheering as well. The long battle was over, and everyone was relieved. Devarius hugged Zaviana, raising her hand high in the air.

Ellisar staggered toward them. His stomach had been bandaged, but he was still weak. He shook Devarius' hand. Ellisar turned to the crowd.

"Everyone!" He coughed. The crowd became silent. "Everyone, congratulations are in order. We defeated the Dragonia Empire. But remember, this war is far from over. This was one battle. And if we don't act soon, they'll recoup and return."

Murmurs began in the crowd once more.

"Saefron is no longer safe," Devarius said.

Ellisar shook his head. "No, no it's not."

"What do we need to do?"

"First, bury the dead. They deserve a proper burial," Ellisar said.

"What about the warriors of the empire?" Zaviana asked.

"Take them outside, pile them up to rot," Ellisar said.

"They're human too."

"Yes, they are. But we don't have time to offer them a burial. I imagine the empire will be back soon. They can bury their own dead. We need to take care of our own, and we need to leave this city."

Devarius nodded.

"People," Ellisar called into the crowd. "Saefron is no longer safe. We cannot stay here. I need everyone to gather their belongings. Tonight, we bury the dead, and we drag the dead bodies of our attackers out of this city. But tomorrow, tomorrow we leave. We cannot wait. We need to rebuild."

Most of the people surrounding them nodded their heads with approval. Some of them scowled as they departed, but most understood.

Devarius was looking forward to leaving Saefron. Truth be told, he was looking forward to returning to Adeth Peak Isle. He missed Aquila. Devarius had left her there to tend the wyvern hatchlings, and because he wanted her safe. He'd lost a lot of friends over the last few days. Grief began to sink in.

Tears filled everyone's eyes. Most were tears of sadness from their lost loved ones, but many others wore tears of joy. They'd won; they'd defeated the empire. However, now they were hurt, and it would take a long time to rebuild. Progress would be slow, and Saefron was lost. They needed to relocate; they needed to train more wyverns.

"How long will it take us to rebuild?" Devarius asked.

Ellisar turned to him. "Rebuild?"

"We lost a lot of men these past few days, Ellisar. Hundreds of them. Many wyverns died as well. We narrowly defeated the empire. However, we were in our own fortified walls. We could never survive a force like that if we struck their stronghold."

"No, we wouldn't."

"When will we be strong enough to fight the empire? I don't mean this hiding and building, I mean actually fight them."

Ellisar shrugged. "I don't know, Devarius. We don't have enough men. We don't have enough allies. But, we won an important battle today. The empire retreats in defeat. I don't know how far they will go, but remember this, their tail is between their legs tonight. Someone will see them. Someone out there will know they lost this battle. They will know the resistance defeated the empire. That is what Galedar has been fearing all along. He doesn't fear the resistance; he doesn't fear the people. He fears hope. We have given the people hope. Now, we'll begin to have real allies, and I'd wager some of them will come from inside the empire's own ranks. We just need to be careful how we tread."

Devarius nodded. "Patience. I know. I'm not good at it."

Ellisar laughed, a loud, rumbling belly laugh. "No, Devarius, you're not. But, that's why I keep you around. I'm slow to action, putting effort first to thought. However, you're quick to action, quick to step in and be the hero. That is what makes you great. People look up to you. And hopefully, all the plans I've made to fight back against the tyranny will finally be put to use through you, through your action."

"Where are the elemental humans?" Devarius asked.

"Elemental humans?" Ellisar asked.

"The men who drank the wyvern oil."

"Ah." Ellisar smiled. "They're resting. They won't recover until tomorrow."

"They're in a coma?" Zaviana asked.

"In a fashion, yes. Just like the shadowmen. They used a lot of energy, a lot of it borrowed. It will take them a while to recover their energy."

"They saved us," Devarius whispered.

"Yes, they did," Ellisar agreed.

"You were right," Devarius said.

Ellisar smiled. "It does not matter who was right or wrong. What matters is that we survived. And that we make the next step before the empire returns. We need to prepare. We need to be ready."

"I'm anxious to return to Adeth Isle," Devarius whispered.

"As am I," Zaviana agreed.

Chapter 41

Devarius looked back at the city. Saefron was now abandoned. He hoped they could come back one day. Everyone who had died lay in an unmarked grave. Men stayed up all night making individual holes for each person. But they hadn't the time to make gravestones. However, their mapmaker did have time to make a map where each person lay. The gravestones would come ... one day. If they ever truly defeated the Dragonia Empire and could return, they would give everyone a headstone. However, no one planned to return to Saefron to live. It was now Adeth Peak Isle. If they ever defeated the empire, they could move back to the land of Kaeldroga, where the people would be happiest. But, never again would it be Saefron.

He looked forward to returning to the island. Devarius wanted to continue training with the wyverns. He wanted to continue to learn how to use the wyvern oil, how to improve his aerial combat. What he truly wanted was freedom. His appetite had tasted revenge. Over the last few days, he'd slaughtered dozens of empire soldiers. But he'd had enough killing. He didn't like killing other men. They were the same. Whether brown, white, or tan, men were men. Devarius hated killing men. He hated what they stood for. All he wanted was for them to see the true corruption of the empire and to think for themselves.

They would arrive at the ships soon. Devarius walked by Zaviana's side. After all these years, he was finally reunited with his sister. He'd thought he'd have to search the entire land of Kaeldroga, even over to Dragonia to find her. But she'd come home. They hadn't had a true home in years, but when they were together ... that was home.

All the men and women of the resistance walked in silence toward the ship. They mourned the death of their loved ones. Devarius understood. Scuffling ahead of him snapped his attention from his thoughts. A woman screamed in the distance. Devarius pushed through the crowd, trying to see what was amiss.

Ellisar stared back at him, a sword protruding from his chest. Blood oozed out of his mouth as he collapsed forward. The emperor, Galedar, stood with a triumphant grin on his face, his sword held steady, blood dripping off of it and onto Ellisar's back.

Devarius unsheathed his sword, charging the man. Everyone parted as Devarius yelled. Galedar raised his eyebrows as Devarius approached him. Devarius' sword slammed into the space where Galedar stood, but he was no longer there. Turning, he searched for the emperor. A shadow disappeared in the corner of his eye. Devarius ran after it. The shadow twisted this way and that, disappearing through the crowd of men.

Galedar was gone. He'd stabbed Ellisar through the chest, then turned into a shadow to flee like a coward. Devarius gritted his teeth. He sheathed his sword and ran back to check on Ellisar. Devarius turned the leader over.

"Ellisar," Devarius whispered.

Ellisar smiled. Blood gurgled from his mouth. He wasn't dead yet ... but it wouldn't be long.

"I'm sorry," Devarius said.

Ellisar shook his head. "You're in charge now, boy."

"Me?" Devarius asked.

Ellisar coughed. More blood spat from his mouth. He nodded.

"Why me?"

"You're the leader everyone needs right now. You will do well."

"I'm no leader," Devarius said. "I don't know what to do next."

"You will do fine."

Devarius shook his head. "What am I supposed to do next? How can we possibly defeat the Dragonia Empire?"

Ellisar's mouth opened, but no words came out.

Devarius leaned closer.

"The dragon stone," Ellisar whispered.

"What?" Devarius asked.

"Find it," Ellisar whispered.

He closed his eyes.

"Wait," Devarius pleaded. "What is the dragon stone? What am I supposed to do with it?"

Ellisar didn't answer.

Devarius checked his neck for a pulse. There was nothing. Ellisar was dead. Devarius stood, running his hands over his close-cropped hair. Ellisar was dead, and now the resistance looked to him for leadership. He closed his eyes, cursing under his breath.

When he opened his eyes, everyone was staring at him. Everyone looked to him for guidance.

"We don't have time to rest. We must reach the ships. Bring Ellisar with us. We'll give him a proper burial at sea. There's no time to waste."

Without another word, he turned away from all the pleading eyes and walked south.

THE END

(If you enjoyed this book, please consider leaving a review)

Continue the Dragonia Chronicles
www.CraigAPrice.com/novels.html[1]

Newsletter
www.CraigAPrice.com/email-list.html[2]

---

1. http://www.CraigAPrice.com/novels.html

2. http://www.CraigAPrice.com/email-list.html

EMPOWERING WOMEN? WOMEN wanting to break away from the male-led government? Read more about these amazon women called the Ikchani in my novella based in the same world as The Crimson Claymore and The Chronicles of Starlyn.

You can get it FREE Here[3]

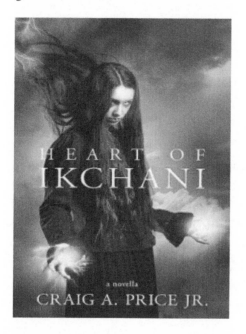

AS AN INDIE AUTHOR, reviews[4] are really important to me. If you enjoyed this story, please leave a Review[5]. I would really appreciate it.

About the Author

Craig A. Price Jr. lives on the Alabama Gulf Coast with his beautiful wife and two sons. He lived in Washington state most of his life, but has also lived in Utah for four years during the winter Olympics. He has full custody of his son, and works full time as a pipefitter. He has finished 7 novels and has seen a lot of success on Wattpad, where his book The Crimson Claymore has seen over 2.5 million reads and was a featured read for over 2 years. On his free time he enjoys to write and read novels, especially of the fantasy genre.

He is your typical fantasy author: He has a beard, a typewriter, he enjoys the occasional tobacco from his long stem pipe, and he loves listening to classical music on his record player.

Read More from Craig A. Price Jr.

www.CraigAPrice.com/novels.html[1]

---

1. http://www.CraigAPrice.com/novels.html